Bite

ISBN # 978-1-78651-354-0

Cover Art by Posh Gosh ©Copyright 2016

Interior text design by Claire Siemaszkiewicz

Totally Bound Publishing

Books by Crissy Smith

Were Chronicles

Pack Alpha
Pack Enforcer
Pack Territory
Pack Rogue
Pack Community
Pack Mates
Pack Daughter
Pack Hunter
Pack Council
Pack Security
Pack Beta
Pack Secrets
Pack Balance
Pack Investigator
Pack Law

Corporate Wolves

The Favour
Losing Control

Secrets

The Shifter and the Dreamer

Shifter Chronicles

Birds of Prey
Bear Claw
Eye of the Tiger

Coyote's Kiss
Wolf Pack

Bloodlines

Bite

Bite Me!

Savage Love

Summer Seductions

Summers' Girl

Cloaks and Daggers

Vampire Hunter

Lust Bites

Seduced by the Neighbour
Fated Love
Bid High
Lacey's Seduction

What's Her Secret?

Designated Alpha
Last Call

Single Titles

Eternal
Magical Ménage
Vamps in the City

Bloodlines

BITE

CRISSY SMITH

Dedication

For my family — who support, encourage, and love me
every single day

Chapter One

Away from the bright lights of the Las Vegas strip, Kieran Smith walked down the dark and litter-ridden street in the roughest part of town. Most tourists didn't see this side of the city but Kieran wasn't like other tourists. He knew he should be in his hotel room steaming in a hot shower or down in the casino spending some of his hard-earned money, but instead he'd strolled for a few hours until he'd found himself far away from the crowds.

Even though the city was well known for sin, there were still different types of vices. The people who had darker and exclusive ones wouldn't be found in the middle of crowds wearing Bermuda shorts with long socks and wielding cameras. No, Kieran had to search out what most people hid from.

He wasn't opposed to sin, necessarily. True he'd spent most of his life protecting those who didn't even know he or his organization existed. But Kieran truly believed that some sins weren't so bad. He strongly believed there were different levels of bad because where was the fun in living if you couldn't enjoy some vices? If he was completely honest with himself, Kieran could admit that he'd left the sanctuary of the safer part of town and was looking for trouble, or more accurately, looking to stop trouble.

He was bored and hadn't seen enough action in the past few weeks. Not since he'd been put on leave along with his partners after an intense case they'd closed with a pack of wolf shifters. Some discreet questioning to the hotel staff where he was staying and Kieran had found where most of the shifters hung around, the ones who caused problems to be more specific. Kieran figured that if any other supernatural types were around, and why wouldn't they be, they'd stay in the same area.

Although he wasn't picky about who or what he captured, his first choice was always shifters. Other than Remy, who'd been one of his work partners for the last several years, Kieran hated all shifters.

If possible, he'd wipe every single one of them off the face of the earth. Unfortunately, as part of the Organization, his job was to protect innocents. It didn't matter if they were human, shifter or like him. Unless they'd committed a crime, they were off limits to him. He really hated that rule.

Kieran had gone through hell when a pack of shifters had captured him after seeing him feed. They'd tortured, experimented on and almost killed him as they'd imprisoned him for over ten years. If it weren't for the Organization getting wind of the lab that had become the only home he could remember, and rescuing him, Kieran knew he wouldn't have made it much longer. Rescue had come but without anywhere to go, he'd been taken in by the people who'd saved him. Although Kieran didn't have the bloodline, like those who were normally chosen to serve as one of the Organization's agents, he'd volunteered to join anyway.

Caspar, the only man who Kieran had trusted for a long time, had put him through training until Kieran had been ready to join the ranks. That was when he'd become partners with Angel, another Day Walker like him, and Remy, the wolf shifter who'd became his best friend. His life had changed due to the Organization, even if everyone other than his boss and two partners thought him crazy. Because of course, he was.

Not only was he a Day Walker that drank blood and fought evil on a daily basis but Kieran was also afraid of the dark, doctors and anything he couldn't control.

All in all, Kieran didn't mind being the psycho of the good guys. He was the monster that parents used in stories to scare their kids into behaving. Only he was very real.

If he hadn't become one of the good guys, there was no telling what he'd have done. So it was a good thing that Caspar had decided he was worth keeping around. Because Kieran would make a really good bad guy, and he knew it.

There were times like tonight when Kieran knew he was standing on the edge between doing the right thing and letting the darkness inside him finally come out. He was barely hanging on to the little sanity he had so he'd gone out hunting for trouble even though he was supposed to be on vacation.

However, after two hours of stalking the streets, Kieran hadn't run into any trouble or even seen another supernatural creature. A few humans were scattered around — most appeared homeless and down on their luck, but there was nothing that required his talents.

Resigned to another night of hanging around the smoky casino floor instead of having any fun, Kieran took the next left at the corner and headed back toward his temporary home. Could a hotel be considered a home? He guessed it didn't really matter. Kieran didn't especially want to be anywhere, so this was as good a place as any. His boss had suggested Las Vegas as one of his vacation spots, thinking that Kieran wouldn't stand out as much here as he normally did. Not that it was Kieran's fault. If they'd wanted him to behave, they shouldn't have sent him on vacation. He didn't care if his partners needed time off. Kieran was lost when he didn't have a purpose.

A scream pierced the quiet night and Kieran froze. He concentrated on the sound to narrow down where it had come from. The empty streets and alleys could cause noise to echo. But Kieran was good at what he did. He took off, using his super-speed to close the distance between him and whoever needed his help. He skidded around an old brick building, which led him into a dark alley. With his excellent night vision, Kieran didn't have any trouble spotting the young couple, a male and female, backed into a wall while three hulking figures closed in on them.

The female screamed again while the attackers laughed at her.

"Hey." Kieran barely raised his voice. If these guys were supernatural, he wouldn't need to. Just as he'd expected, they turned toward him while still keeping their prey in their sights. "Having a party?" Kieran asked with his friendliest tone.

The biggest of the three, an ugly mountain of a man, snarled at him.

Kieran sniffed. It was shifters he'd deal with tonight, oh goody. Kieran could scent the animal part of them clearly. They smelled like wet cat, so feline shifters were on the menu. Depending on what species they were, Kieran could probably figure on a pretty damn good fight. He rubbed his hands together in anticipation.

"Get lost," Mountain Man warned him. He was scenting Kieran and frowning. The shifter wouldn't be able to figure out why Kieran didn't carry any smell except for what he'd picked up from his environment. It was also fun when his opposition had no idea what he was. "Now," the man grumbled.

"I can't do that," Kieran replied with cheer. "I don't think your friends wanted an invite but I do."

"Mind your own business," a second man, small, face like a rat, demanded.

Kieran laughed. "Damn, I don't think I've seen three uglier men in my life. And I've lived a pretty long time." He was giving them hints that he wasn't just another human. With witnesses he couldn't reveal his true nature. His kind wasn't well known and there was a reason for that.

The youngest looking, who had chocolate puppy-dog eyes, was the only one who appeared wary of him. Kieran moved forward slowly the entire time he taunted the shifters, and the youngest was stepping back. Now he was only about six feet away. He glanced over at the couple who were watching him with wide eyes. He waved his hand to them. "Come here," he ordered.

The woman started toward him but the rat man stepped in front of her. "I don't think so. They're ours."

"Not anymore," Kieran said. He leaped up and over the heads of the attackers. He knew he'd taken them by surprise when he was able to shove the rat man forward, sending him flying. Puppy Dog was the first to move but instead of coming at Kieran, he jumped back. Kieran grinned. "I'd get out of here if you don't want to get really hurt," Kieran advised.

Mountain Man growled and lunged at him. Kieran evaded his meaty hand and kicked out, catching his attacker in the knee. The big man went down. That was when the others came at him at the same time. Guess Puppy Dog had grown balls or at least enough to team up with Rat Man. Kieran's training took over. He yelled for the couple to run while he blocked, punched and fought until he was the only one standing. Breathing heavily, he rested his hands on his knees as he stood over his three fallen foes.

That had been fun. He pulled out his phone and hit the pre-dialed number for dispatch. "Clean up on aisle two," he said when the call connected.

"Damn it, Kieran," Lettie Sanchez muttered in his ear. "You're supposed to be on vacation."

"I am on vacation," he argued. "It's not my fault this time."

Lettie snorted. "Trouble just finds you? More like you go looking for it."

It was scary how well Lettie and his other friends knew him. He didn't respond since he really couldn't deny her claim without lying, and he always tried to tell the truth no matter what the circumstances were. He had enough negative traits without adding being a liar as well.

"I've traced the GPS on your phone and am calling in the local agents. Are the suspects secured?" Lettie questioned.

Kieran nudged the ribs of Mountain Man with the toe of his black combat book. "I don't think they're going to be a problem."

"They're not dead, are they?"

He chuckled. "No, there's too much paperwork for dead bodies." And wasn't that the truth. He could remember when the Organization hadn't been so picky about how he took care of threats. But now, they'd gone all politically correct and shit. He suspected that the new views had something to do with the fact that the shifters had gone public and now everyone knew about them. That wasn't something that he worried too much about, though. Above his pay grade.

"How many?" Lettie asked.

"Three," he said with some pride. Kieran might be one of the oldest agents, even if he appeared to be in his early thirties, but he still had it. He could still throw down with the best of them.

Lettie sighed heavily. "When is Angel returning from her honeymoon? She's the only one who can deal with your crazy ass."

"Not for another two weeks," Kieran answered. "Guess you're stuck with me until then."

"Where's Remy?" Lettie questioned. "Sometimes he can be a good influence." Which was sort of true. Mostly, though, Kieran ended up getting both him and Remy in trouble.

"We're on vacation," Kieran reminded her. "He's home with his pack. I'm spending all my money at the tables."

"If that was the case, you wouldn't be calling me to clean up another one of your messes," Lettie pointed out.

Kieran strolled away from the men, who were out cold and who would no doubt remain that way until others arrived. He jumped up and landed on the edge of a graffiti-painted concrete wall before he sat to wait. "You could come down and keep me company."

"Oh, what a wonderful offer. Not," Lettie teased. "I haven't done anything to deserve that kind of punishment."

The banter between them was familiar and finished out

his night pretty well. Lettie had been around about half the time he had but they'd connected from the start. She loved electronics as much as he did and was always showing him new inventions she'd come up with. Kieran always took them out to the field and tested them for her. All without their boss knowing because he wouldn't be happy.

"I hear a vehicle approaching," he said. "I'll catch you later, babe." He hung up before she could respond but that was usual for him and he secretly thought Lettie enjoyed his antics.

Kieran stayed where he was, high on the fence, hidden in the dark. A black SUV with heavily tinted windows rolled into the alley. With the headlights bright into the small space, the bodies would be easily seen. Both doors opened, the driver male and passenger female exiting.

"Fuck," the man cursed. When he moved away from the open door, he had his weapon drawn. He was staring at the three men laid out.

Kieran had to smile. He'd enjoy fucking with this agent.

The woman was more cautious. She slowly walked to the front of the vehicle but her eyes were darting around the alley. She wasn't looking at the attackers but instead for who had taken them down. He respected that vigilance. It was what he would do.

He silently rose as he watched. They hadn't spotted him yet. The man was human but the woman was a shifter. It was hard not to snarl at her but he managed. Kieran bent his knees before he leaped down. He landed between them with a loud thud. He ducked slightly when both weapons were pointed at his head. He held up his hands. "Don't shoot," he mocked.

"Kieran Smith." The man lowered his weapon. "I've heard about you, been warned really."

Kieran grinned then glanced at the woman since she hadn't lowered her weapon. "Gonna shoot me?"

"I haven't decided, like my partner said, we've heard about you," she said.

He couldn't really argue with her logic. "Just don't aim for my face. It's too pretty to be shot off."

It was slight but he saw her lips twitch in amusement. And what lips they were—full, plump and red. *Shit!* Where had that thought come from? There was no way in hell that he'd ever find a shifter attractive. Even if the shifter in question had a curvy body, long brown hair streaked with red, and gorgeous bright gold eyes. He'd never seen that color before, but no matter what, Kieran would not think she was hot. No, no way would he ever find a shifter sexy.

"So what happened here?" the male agent asked.

"These three assholes had a couple up against the wall." He waved his hand back as he spoke. "I came along and showed them the error of their ways."

"You took on three shifters all by yourself?" she questioned in disbelief as she strolled closer to the men on the floor. She bent and sniffed.

Kieran grinned. "I thought you'd heard of me?" Lettie had either warned the two agents about him or his reputation was growing. Kieran wasn't sure which he preferred.

"Okay, on that note, I'm Dean Westbridge and this is my partner, Dakota Reese, and we'll be taking over here."

"Dean and Dakota, that's so cute!" Kieran couldn't help but say. Did the Organization chapter here put agents together alphabetically?

Dean snorted. "You really are an asshole."

"Well, Dean Westbridge…" Kieran stopped. *Westbridge?* "Ah fuck!"

"Maybe you're not as slow as you seem," Dakota commented as she rolled the Mountain Man over and secured his hands behind his back with plastic cuffs.

Kieran peered back at Dean, unsure of his next action. *Things just got real interesting.*

The Organization ran off bloodlines. That was how agents were chosen and why they were able to remain secret. The first born, male or female, were sent into service, and very rarely was anyone else ever allowed to even know about their existence. The Westbridges were one of the original families who had formed the Organization. It was also the bloodline that Caspar had been born into. Part of an agreement the founders had made centuries ago. So Dean was related to Kieran's boss—the man he loved like a father. This wasn't good. He'd been hoping to avoid being on Caspar's radar while he was supposed to be taking time off.

"By the look on your face, I'm guessing you've figured out who my uncle is," Dean said. "And if I'm remembering the last conversation I had with him, Caspar told me that you would be in town and to keep an eye on you."

Like he needed a fucking babysitter? Kieran scowled. "Then you haven't been doing a very good job," he taunted. "I've been in town for several days and haven't seen you until tonight."

"But that doesn't mean I haven't seen you. Or how you drink way too much at the hotel bar before dropping several hundred dollars at blackjack?"

"I'm a gambler at heart," he quipped. How hadn't he seen this man watching him? Well actually, Kieran knew. He didn't give humans a second look. They were no threat to him. Kieran was untouchable. Or at least he'd always believed he was. This human male might be a challenge. Kieran turned his back to Dean, showing him that he didn't find him any danger. Dakota had bound the mountain man, the rat guy, and was now bending over the young puppy-dog-eyed kid.

Kieran strolled over to her with his hands in the pockets of his dark jeans. "That one's not much more than a kid. He couldn't fight off a tick. Do shifters get fleas and ticks?" he baited her.

Dakota glanced up at him. "Could you be any more obvious?" she asked.

He lifted an eyebrow.

"Fine." She finished securing the attacker then stood. "You can continue to play your games and push away everyone you meet. If that's the way you want to play it, we can't stop you. But maybe you should ask yourself why Caspar suggested you take the rest of your vacation here?"

"He likes to screw with my head," he replied with a shrug.

"Sure." She patted his chest before resting her palm over his heart.

The heat from her hand seeped through his cotton T-shirt and he froze. For the first time in many years, his instinct was not to rip off the head of the shifter who touched him. Instead he ached to pull her close. He shook his head to gather control of himself.

"I can see you've got this under control," he murmured. Then he sped off. Kieran put every ounce of his energy in getting away from Dakota.

He had a hotel to check out of and another lodging to find. Dean might have been given the task of watching out for him but Kieran wouldn't make it easy for him.

So let the games begin.

Dakota grinned as Kieran disappeared almost right before her eyes. "Damn, he's fast."

"And you need to be careful. Caspar specifically told us that Kieran hates shifters and that he'd like nothing more than to kill you," Dean told her. "You shouldn't have touched him."

Probably, but she hadn't been able to help herself. It was so obvious that Kieran used his sharp tongue to push others away. He didn't want people close to him but there was also a longing for connection deep inside him that she could sense. It was her job to read people—what she'd specialized in during training. Kieran Smith was so much more than what he appeared.

"Maybe you should stay away from him. I can have Gabe help me follow him," Dean said.

"No." While Kieran might have issues, it hadn't been hate that she'd seen in his eyes. The spark of attraction had been unmistakable. He wasn't exactly what she'd been expecting either so she'd paid attention to every detail. "I'm not backing off."

When she'd touched him, he'd been shocked. Kieran's body had been hard and cool but his eyes had been full of heat.

"Shit," Dean muttered. "You have that look on your face."

"What look?" she asked with fake innocence.

"The one that says you've found a lost puppy to bring home," he said.

She'd laugh, but he wasn't too far off. Kieran needed to know that someone cared for him. He was lost in his own world and very alone. It wasn't in Dakota to leave someone to flounder about. The fact that she was attracted to him just added to her need to care for him. Whether he liked it or not.

A groan sounded from behind as she whirled around. The biggest of the shifters was waking up. "Let's get these guys processed so we can get back to your secret mission," she said.

"I can't believe I let Caspar talk me into watching him," Dean bitched.

"Like you'd ever say no to Caspar," she said. Caspar was better to Dean than Dean's own father. Because of the respect Dean had for his uncle, there was no doubt that he'd do anything Caspar asked. "You know he'll be gone by the time we get done here and back to his hotel."

"Yeah," Dean agreed. "Let's get these three loaded and I'll call Gabe to stake him out. He won't leave town so we'll find him."

"Maybe," Dakota said, not really agreeing. Now that Kieran knew they were watching him, there was no telling what he would do. She didn't think he'd just disappear, though. His personality made her think he'd try to make it really hard to keep their promise to watch him. Kieran would probably do his best to show them up.

"I'll get the little guy," Dean said as he walked to the youngest of their prisoners.

"Thanks," she grumbled as she strode to the largest man, and the only one who was awake. "Hey." She lightly kicked his side. "Get up."

The man scowled at her. "Who the fuck are you?"

Dakota dropped to her knees in front of him. She let her jaguar come close to the surface. She had a powerful animal inside her, and the way the guy's eyes widened, she knew he hadn't been prepared for the wave of dominance that she released. "Any more questions?" she growled.

He shook his head.

As she climbed to her feet, she grabbed his arm and hauled him up. Dean had already carried the smallest to the back of their SUV and was now headed in her direction. She pushed her detainee toward Dean before turning to the last guy. He was scrawny and damn ugly. No wonder he'd turned to a life of crime. Dakota bent to lift him up and threw him over her shoulder.

Dean just shook his head at her. It was an ongoing joke between them that she did most of the heavy lifting and that he was the brains in their partnership. Sure, it had something to do with her shifter strength, but really Dakota enjoyed showing off her muscles and Dean was really smart. They worked well together.

She carried the last suspect to the SUV, then Dean helped her get him inside.

"You drive," Dean said as he circled around the back of the vehicle. "I'll make the phone calls to track down our wayward Walker." It was the first time Dean had brought up what Kieran was.

"Have you ever met a Walker before now?" she asked as she slammed the back door shut. She climbed into the driver's seat and started the SUV.

"No," Dean said as he joined her. "There are just so few of them. My dad, and of course Caspar, talks about some of the older ones but I've never come face to face with anyone like Kieran before."

She hadn't either. "I've read a lot of reports involving Day

Walkers," she said. "I wonder how much is true and how much they put into the reports to keep their secrets."

"I would think if the information comes from our files, it would be pretty accurate," Dean told her.

"I don't know," she argued. "Wouldn't it make more sense to only put in the details they don't mind us knowing about?"

"They've been around too long for the Organization not to know almost everything," he told her.

"Okay." She put their SUV into reverse and started to back out of the alley. She still thought her partner was wrong but only time would tell. The more she could watch Kieran, the better idea she would have about how Walkers worked.

Beside her, Dean was speaking to Gabe about arranging a more detailed surveillance on Kieran. Gabe worked on a team with Dare, a bear shifter, and Riley, a fox shifter. Their team backed her and Dean the most. There were currently four squads of agents in the Las Vegas area. Her boss, Marcello Sparro, had concerns about the number of supernaturals who were arriving in town. There was talk about recruiting more agents.

Secretly that was the reason that Kieran had been directed to vacation here. Dakota didn't know why Caspar wouldn't just tell Kieran what was going on. Instead Caspar had told Kieran he needed time off, and told Dean to keep an eye on the Walker. She wondered what else they didn't know.

As she drove south, heading to the Organization headquarters, she kept her eye out for Kieran. There was a good chance that he might follow them. To her knowledge, Kieran didn't know where their office was located, and that information would be beneficial to him to find if he was planning anything against them. It wasn't like he'd be able to type them into a Google search or look for them in the phone book. They didn't exist to the outside world.

While the general public might be aware that shifters existed, they had no clue what still remained in the shadows. Day Walkers were the closest thing to what people would call vampires. Yes, Walkers drank blood, had superior senses and were the scariest in the supernatural world, but they were also the rarest. And all the myths about vampires and how to kill them were pretty much bullshit from what her research had shown. Crosses, garlic and wooden stakes had no more control over them than they would on a human or shifter.

It was interesting the way humans had accepted shifters easily enough and yet had never thought to ask what else was out there.

Dakota made a left on Falcon Ave, which would lead her right into the underground parking garage of the Murphy Institute — the cover corporation for the Las Vegas Organization's units.

The Murphy Institute took half a block and rose three stories high. The dark brick hid one of the most advanced businesses in the country. Everything inside, from the labs, temporary housing and lock-up to the sleek offices were all state of the art. It could be a little intimidating the first time someone walked through the doors but Dakota loved it there. It sure as hell beat her training days of camping out for months at a time, constant cold and wetness, and the dorms she'd grown up living in.

Unlike most of her coworkers, Dakota lived on site. She didn't see the point of getting her own place, since at any time she could be sent away for a temporary assignment or for a permanent relocation. Why get comfortable when in a second she could be gone? Her partner was the total opposite but he had more contact with his family than most agents.

Dakota hadn't spoken to her parents or siblings since she was a teenager. It was just too hard to hear about how well her family was doing when she'd never be allowed to join them. She had five siblings, two of whom she'd never even met. Not that she didn't keep an eye on them, but she kept it strictly to her files and under surveillance. She made no effort to contact them and they didn't even seem to think about her, ever.

She shook her depressing thoughts away. This was her life, and for the most part, she enjoyed what she did. As the eldest child, it was her duty to follow the agreement that her ancestors had made. She was a third-generation agent and her family depended on her to watch out for the innocent.

"We're here," she told Dean as she slowed to a stop at the guard gate leading into the underground parking. Her vehicle was equipped with a tracking device and a bar scan on the window so the sensors could pick her up, but she still had to show her ID to get inside.

She rolled down her window before she flipped open her identification. "Hey, Margie," she greeted the guard on duty.

"Hi, Dakota, Dean." Margie walked up to the driver side. She peered in the back. "Three?" she asked.

"Yes," Dakota confirmed. "We'll take them directly to the third-floor lock-up."

Since the shifter suspects had targeted humans, her and Dean's job was to get them processed so the law-enforcement agents could be informed. They'd call in either the local police or use the newly formed Shifter Coalition, depending on how severe the crime was. With these three jokers, Dakota guessed it would be the locals who would have to come pick them up.

The Shifter Coalition worked more like the FBI or Homeland Security but was run entirely by shifters. Their presence was common knowledge as shifters had publically started the agency so that humans knew nonhumans were being policed as well. Dakota had only met a couple of Coalition agents since they'd opened an office close by but those she'd met seemed to be good people. It didn't bother her that they were in her town. It actually helped. While the Coalition took the more public cases and had to work within human laws, Dakota and the Organization could continue to slink around in the shadows.

"This is it," she said to her passengers.

"Where are we and what in the hell was that man earlier? He wasn't a shifter and he sure wasn't human," the big guy asked.

Dakota glanced up into the rear-view mirror so she could see his eyes. "This is the final stop of our tour. You'll be passed off to the cops from here."

"Cops!" he shouted. "I should be the one pressing charges. That man was a lunatic."

"That man could have killed you and no one would have ever known," Dakota said honestly. "Instead he called for us to pick you up. You should count yourself lucky."

The prisoner snorted. "Yeah right."

"And if you know what's good for you," Dean added, looking over into the back seat, "you'll make sure your paths never cross again."

Dakota pressed her lips tight to hide her smile. The way all three prisoners paled spoke volumes.

"What was he?" the youngest looking asked in a whisper.

"You best pray you never find out," she warned.

He nodded frantically.

Chapter Two

"No, Remy," Kieran growled into the phone. "I do not need you to come up here and keep an eye on me."

"I didn't say keep an eye on you. I just thought you might want some company," Remy argued.

"I don't," Kieran said firmly.

"Yeah right." Remy snorted. "That's why you went hunting earlier?"

Kieran didn't know who Remy had heard that from but he'd put his money on Lettie. The woman never had learned to mind her own business. He'd call her on it but Lettie would just cluck at him and probably wouldn't let him play with her newest toys if he pissed her off too much. "I was just in the neighborhood. Now I'm back at my hotel and getting into the shower."

That was sort of the truth. He'd gone straight back to the room he'd gotten when he'd arrived in town but he'd quickly packed his things and sneaked out. His hotel had been off Strip but he'd decided it would be better to hide in plain sight. He'd moved to a better-known place right in the middle of the action. It would make it harder for Caspar's spies to find him. Give Kieran time to start stalking them first. But he did plan to take a shower, so he wasn't actually lying.

"Come on, K," Remy whined. "I like Vegas."

"You like all the pretty lights and sexy woman," Kieran replied. "You hate the crowds, noise and smells of the big city. Just stay with your family and turn into a furry beast. I don't need you here."

Remy sighed. "Fine, but if you get into any trouble, you

know our boss will send me anyway so you better be on your best behavior."

Okay, so hunting hadn't been the greatest of ideas, but he'd found out Caspar had put babysitters on him so it hadn't been totally wasted. "Caspar won't hear a peep from me," he promised. As long as he could keep Dean off his trail—and that shouldn't be too hard—he figured he could stay under the radar. Maybe he'd call his boss and tell him he was moving on. No, Caspar would grow suspicious. He'd just bide his time and watch those who were supposed to be watching him.

Kieran could hear a lot of racket coming from Remy's side of the phone.

"Remind me again why I came home?" Remy asked, sounding frustrated.

"You love your family," Kieran answered him. A wolf shifter needed pack, and it was hard for Remy to be on his own. Kieran figured that was why they'd become such good friends. Remy's shifter side craved the closeness of others.

"I'll stay a couple more days but maybe I'll join you for the last week. I need a vacation from my vacation."

"Okay," Kieran laughed. "That'll work." He just had to get rid of Dean and that sexy shifter first. *No! Damn it, Dakota is not sexy, she's an animal.* And the only animal that Kieran could ever stand was his best friend.

"I've got to go," Remy said as a woman shouted his name. "Call me if you need anything." He hung up before Kieran could respond.

Kieran shook his head as he placed his phone on the nightstand next to his king-size bed. He'd checked into one of the nicest suites that the hotel had to offer. The room had a large bedroom with an adjoining bathroom, a living area with a wet bar, flat-screen television, a smaller dining area, and a good-sized kitchen. It was a lot more expensive than the room that he'd left but it was luxurious, which he appreciated.

He hadn't checked out of his old room, keeping the charges open on his company card. If his purchases were being monitored, this suite wouldn't be found. He'd used his personal card under a false identity that he had set up many years ago. He'd learned a trick or two in his time with the Organization. Not even Remy or Angel would be able to track him down now.

The staff had brought up the extra blankets and pillows he'd requested and dinner should arrive in another half an hour. Kieran piled the bed with the extra covers and pillows, making a soft and comfortable nest much like his bed at home.

Since his body ran cooler than a human's, Kieran preferred to sleep buried in the coziness of blankets. It was something he allowed himself that very few people knew about. He was old enough to know craving comfort wasn't really a weakness but Kieran wasn't used to sharing any part of himself at all. It was hard for him to accept that what others learned about him wouldn't be used later to hurt him. Only his partners knew his secret but he was sure they'd take it to the grave. Kieran finished throwing the covers on then sauntered to the bathroom.

White tiles and dark-green marble covered the walls, floor and shower stall. There was a vanity with two sinks and plenty of counter space. He'd already unpacked his bag and set his toiletries out. Next to the large glass shower was a huge sunken-in Jacuzzi tub. He might relax in there later but at the moment he just wanted to wash the scent of sweat and city off him. Getting Dakota's shifter's smell off him would also help him relax. It was barely there, but Dakota's sweet aroma seemed to haunt him.

He turned the water on hot before he began to strip off his clothes. He'd throw them into the dry-cleaning bag provided on the back of the bathroom door and would have them cleaned later. He did enjoy not having to find a laundromat and washing his own clothes. Maybe he should have a hotel to live in when he returned home. Nah, too many people around, and he'd get tired of it.

Once naked, he stepped into the shower and groaned as the water cascaded over his shoulders. Three different shower heads rained a refreshing stream over him and it felt amazing. He grabbed the shower gel he'd set on the ledge earlier and poured some into his hand. He quickly scrubbed his body then went about washing his hair. It felt good to be clean again, and the only scent he could now pick up was the light spice from his soap.

He was probably cutting it close to the time his dinner would arrive but Kieran had one more piece of business to take care of. He grabbed his body wash again and added more to his hand before he gripped his hard shaft. Even though he could no longer pick up on Dakota's orange and cinnamon fragrance that had clung to him since she'd touched him, his cock was still rock hard. And what the hell had been up with that? No one touched him—ever. Not even his two partners, who he was closer to than anyone else.

Just remembering the heat from her hand had him closing his eyes while leaning back against the wet tiles. Kieran ran his thumb over the head of his cock before he stroked down. The heat from the shower helped warm him but he wondered if Dakota's palm would heat him up in the same way if her hand replaced his. He gasped as the thought had his balls aching and his cock twitching.

Kieran had slept with plenty of humans after he'd joined the Organization. Shifters? That was different. What those animals had done to him in captivity could not be called sex.

No! He wouldn't think about them. Not when he was hard and ready to come. Kieran tightened his grip as he reached down with his other hand and started to tug gently on his balls. *Oh fuck, that feels good.* Faster, rougher, he jacked himself off. If Dakota were in the shower with him, this would be the moment he would push her down to her knees. Yes, he could picture himself stroking off with

Dakota in front of him with her mouth open. He'd position the head of his cock at her mouth... He grunted as he came. Kieran kept rubbing his shaft until his seed covered the tiled floor and was washed away.

He turned toward the water and rinsed off.

Now that he was clean, sated and relaxed, he was starving. He hoped his food would arrive soon. He turned off the faucets before he grabbed a white fluffy towel off the warmer.

Ah, he moaned as he dragged the fabric over his body. He finished off by scrubbing his hair with it. Once he was dry, he dropped the towel into the pile with his clothes and strolled back into the bedroom. He picked up a pair of thick pajama bottoms and pulled them on as a knock sounded at the suite door.

"Dinner," he said hopefully. He walked out of the bedroom and into the main living area. Before another knock sounded, he opened the door and waved the room service attendant inside. "Please set it up on the table."

The young man nodded, not even looking twice at Kieran answering the door in only sleep pants. Kieran watched as the human carefully set the covered dish and carafe of coffee on the dark, square table. Kieran didn't see anything suspicious in the man's actions so he relaxed. He did take a deep breath so he could remember the man's scent later if he did need to find the human again. Just precaution, he told himself.

The dark-haired human finished then turned the cart around and wheeled it toward Kieran. "If you'll sign this, please, sir." He held out a black leather pouch.

Kieran added a generous tip then scrawled his false name. The human slipped it behind his back then nodded and pushed the cart toward the door, which Kieran still held open.

"Have a good night, sir."

"Thank you," Kieran murmured.

Once the attendant was gone, Kieran locked back up

before he strode over to the table. He removed the silver dome, revealing his rare steak, loaded baked potato, carrots with cheese sauce, green beans and rolls. There was a crystal glass filled with ice water along with an empty mug. The carafe of coffee smelled strong and fresh and he quickly poured himself some.

He took a deep breath, pulling in all the mouthwatering aromas. He loved food and even though his late-night order would cost him hundreds, it was worth it. Kieran sat down and arranged his food. Rarely did a Day Walker have to take blood. His existence was nothing like movies or books showed. He didn't hunt down prey and drink them dry. As a matter of fact, the older a Walker, the less blood they needed.

The line about him being undead was also complete bullshit. His heart still pumped, blood continued to flow, and his cock still worked. Still, humans loved to think of them as demons or something like that when in reality he had a rare blood disease. He, as well as all Day Walkers, had a poison in his body that he'd been born with. The bad blood ate up the good blood and he had to replenish the good blood by drinking from others. Just a few sips every couple of weeks or even a month. The more he exerted himself, the faster he had to drink but Kieran knew how to manage his body.

Kieran picked up his fork and knife and started to cut up his steak. Oh man, it was cooked perfectly. He mopped up some of the juices that escaped with a fatty piece before he popped the meat in his mouth. He moaned and stabbed another.

Maybe he did need to think about moving into a hotel after all. This was the best meal he'd had in ages. He tried some of the potato then carrots. As he ate, he reached over to his laptop and turned it on. As it loaded, he thought about what he wanted to look up. Every agent had some level of access but personal files were off limits. Although he did know someone who could easily get the information that he wanted. He just needed to find something that he could bribe Lettie with.

Oh, he had just the thing. If he could get to his storage unit in Utah and grab the box that he'd hidden over twenty years ago, Lettie would go nuts. Or maybe, just maybe, he could call a friend. Remy was close to his storage unit and would have to pass by on his way to Nevada. That would be perfect.

He finished the rest of his food before he jogged into the bedroom where he'd left his phone. He sent a quick text to Remy, who responded right away that he'd be happy to grab something for him on the way. Kieran guessed now he wouldn't have a choice whether or not his partner joined him. Oh well, he'd take Remy out on the town and introduce him to a couple of beautiful women. That would distract his friend long enough for Kieran to take care of the other agents. It wasn't like he was going to hurt them. But a wild goose chase could be fun. He wondered what they'd do if they knew how much trouble he was about to go to in order for them to chase their tails.

Grinning, Kieran found Lettie's personal number in his contacts and hit the Call button. This vacation might turn out to be the best he'd ever taken.

* * * *

Low jazz music played as Dakota sipped her drink. She'd been sitting in the small bar inside Kieran's hotel for over an hour, waiting for him to leave his suite. It was almost two in the morning and at some point she would have to head home to get some sleep. She still had a job to do even if they were taking shifts keeping an eye on Kieran. Maybe he was in for the night?

Their plan had worked perfectly since Gabe had witnessed Kieran leaving the other hotel and had followed him here. They'd even confirmed he was inside the suite he'd rented in another name by sending Gabe in to deliver a meal. The others had all left, since it appeared that Kieran was probably not leaving again. Dakota wasn't so sure. As keyed up as she was, Kieran had to be feeling close to the same.

It was better that everyone else had gone home, though. The conversation she wanted to have with Kieran was of a personal nature that didn't need to be overheard.

She could go up to his room and knock, show him that they knew where he was. No, she'd rather he came to her. Dakota set her glass on the tabletop and stood, preparing to leave.

Kieran walked in.

With a smile, she sat once again and leaned back, hoping to come across as confident and relaxed even as her pulse sped up. He looked good in a pair of dark jeans and a black sweater that appeared soft. Kieran glanced around the bar before his gaze settled on her. He jerked a little but smoothly covered it as he narrowed his eyes at her. If she hadn't been watching closely, she would never have seen his shock. Dakota picked up her drink and tipped it at him.

Kieran's lips moved but she couldn't hear what he said, which was probably best since he couldn't be saying anything good as he glared at her. Dakota crooked her finger at him.

He stalked across the bar floor, and she admired the way he moved. Kieran was tall—at least six feet two but he moved with a grace that she had to attribute to his species. She wasn't certain, since she'd never met another Walker, but just watching him, she could see the power of his body being restrained. Inside, her jaguar woke and came alive. Her training had taught her how to keep her shifter side close so she'd always be prepared to defend herself. Because of this her normal hazel eyes turned gold and she had the instincts of a jaguar that she had to contend with.

As much as she wanted to rub against Kieran's leg and mark him with her scent, Dakota was pretty sure the Walker wouldn't like that so she restrained herself. "Buy you a drink?" she asked once he'd reached her.

"How'd you find me?" he asked as he took the seat across from her.

Dakota smiled. "Now I can't reveal all my secrets," she said. "But I can buy you a drink."

He finally sighed then nodded.

"Oh good," she said as she lifted her hand to call over the waiter.

"Another whiskey sour?" the waiter asked.

"Yes please," she replied.

"And for you, sir?" the waiter asked.

Kieran's lips twitched. "The same."

"I'll have them right out," he promised.

Dakota waited until the waiter walked away before she peered over at Kieran with a raised eyebrow.

"What?" he snapped. "So we drink the same. That doesn't mean anything." He was going to fight her every step of the way.

"I thought maybe we could talk," she said.

"About what?" he sniped. His crystal-blue eyes were sharp and suspicious.

"About why you're hiding from everyone," she stated. "Why you don't like shifters."

He stiffened. "What do you know about that?" The change in him was scary. As he spoke his voice lowered and his eyes grew cold.

Dakota swallowed hard.

He moved fast and had ahold of her hand before she could avoid him. Kieran pulled her closer, his grip tight. "What do you know?"

"Nothing," she told him. "Caspar just told us that you didn't like shifters and I needed to be careful."

"And he didn't tell you why?" Kieran questioned.

"No," she said as she tugged to try to dislodge his grasp.

"How is this you being careful?" he asked. "You touch me? You stalk me? You tempt me?"

Oh yes, she did. "So you admit you're tempted?"

"You just don't give up," he said but he did finally release her. "You have no idea what I can do to you."

She ran her finger over his wrist and felt his pulse jump. "So you go from suspicious, to angry, and now back to cocky."

"I'm a mystery." Kieran finished off his drink.

"You're something," she agreed.

"And you think you can figure me out? Better people have tried," he told her. "Also, I don't have the time or inclination to play with you."

"I think you do," she argued. He'd sat with her and was engaging in conversation. If Kieran really weren't interested, then he could have just walked away, but he hadn't.

Kieran grinned, flashing her some fangs. She wasn't sure if he'd done it to intimidate her or if he was hungry. She really needed to learn more about Walkers. There had to be some more intel that was available.

"If I did, do you really believe I'd tell you?" he asked.

Now they were getting somewhere. "If we're keeping score, I believe that I'm in the lead." She spotted their waiter and signaled to get another round.

He nodded discreetly. Dakota scooted her chair closer to him, pleased when Kieran didn't comment or move away.

"Perhaps you are," he said, leaning forward. "But I might be the type of player that enjoys coming from behind."

"I might enjoy that," she teased while brushing her arm against his. The electric spark from the touch surprised her and she gasped. Kieran also jumped.

"What was that?" she asked.

With wide eyes he just stared at her.

"Kieran?"

"I don't know," he admitted. "That's never happened before."

"Huh, that's interesting." Dakota pushed the sleeve of his sweater up as she kept her gaze on his.

Kieran remained still but allowed her to run her palm

over his bare arm. Again she felt a slight shock. "Wow," she murmured as she continued to stroke his forearm. Kieran shuddered briefly and his eyelids fluttered. His skin was cool to the touch. She'd never felt anything like this.

The waiter set down two more glasses then disappeared. Dakota never took her eyes off Kieran, caught in the depths of his gaze.

"Kieran," she said softly. He leaned forward and grazed his cheek against hers. She moaned then tightened her fingers over his wrist.

"Finish your drink and let's go upstairs," he whispered.

Her breath caught at the glow of his blue eyes. It was amazing and very nonhuman. She lifted her hand to sweep her thumb across his eyebrow.

"Scared?" he asked in a challenging tone, but Dakota could feel his insecurity. Deep down, Kieran wanted to be accepted but no one had been able to gain that absolute trust with him. She doubted Kieran himself even knew how badly he craved the connection.

"I'm not scared—intrigued and needy, but I'm not afraid of you," she assured him.

"Let's go then," he said as he stood.

Dakota hopped up and reached for her purse.

"I've got it," Kieran said as he dropped a couple of large bills on the table.

"No, I said I'd buy you a drink," she tried to push his hand away.

"I've already done it," he told her as he held out his hand. "Are you coming or not?"

Dakota placed her palm inside his. "Yes."

He tugged her after him then they were strolling across the floor. She wondered what he was thinking as he led her away. He wanted her—that much was obvious—but they'd gone from challenging each other to rushing upstairs.

When she'd entered the bar, somehow she'd missed the private elevator close by. Kieran strolled straight to it as he pulled his key card out of his pocket. He swiped the card through the reader and the elevator doors opened instantly. Kieran pushed her in ahead of him, and as soon as the doors whooshed closed, he was on her.

His lips clamped down on hers as he gripped her waist. Dakota wrapped her arms around his back and held him close. He devoured her and she loved every minute. The electric current that ran between them traveled down her spine until she was crazy with need. She lifted her leg over his hip then dug her heel into his leg as he rutted against her.

She needed so bad. It had never felt like this before. The intensity of passion between them made her so damn hot. She wanted to tear off their clothes and she really didn't care who might see.

Kieran ripped his mouth away and peered down at her with his eyes glazing. "The things I'm going to do to you tonight will make your head spin."

His fangs were even more visible. "Bring it on," she said as she yanked him forward again.

The elevator dinged before their lips could connect once more. Kieran laughed as he grasped her other leg and hefted her up. She was used to being the strong one in the relationship, professional and private, and it felt good to be able to depend on someone else.

He carried her out of the elevator and down the hall. Since his neck was right there Dakota licked a strip from his neck up behind his ear. He stumbled but quickly righted himself. Oh looky, she'd found a hot spot. She licked again but this time added a scrape of her teeth.

He groaned as he backed her into a wall. His lips covered hers, and she opened to grant him access. While his tongue brushed against hers and explored the inside of her mouth, she clawed at the back of his sweater. She wanted naked, skin-to-skin contact.

"I have to get the door open," he panted against her lips.

"Hurry," she urged. Dakota managed to get her hands under his sweater and splayed her palms against his back.

The muscles strained as he fumbled with the card reader.

"Hang on," he ordered, then they were through the door. She squeaked as he moved so fast that she couldn't follow where they were headed. Damn, she'd known he was fast, but to actually feel it? That was so cool!

He stopped but her body wasn't prepared. She tilted to the side, and he laughed as he dropped her onto the soft mattress. Dakota was almost buried inside a cocoon of blankets on the bed. Kieran climbed up and straddled her waist. He buried his hands in her hair and tugged, exposing her neck.

Kieran dropped his head, covering her pulse there with his lips. He sucked and she reached up to grab his arms where they bracketed her head. She wasn't afraid, just needed to touch him. To show him that he didn't scare her, Dakota arched up to touch more of his body.

Would he bite her? Drink from her? She didn't care if he did. Dakota was going to prove to Kieran that not all shifters needed to be feared or would hurt him. She might not know what had happened in his past but someone, a shifter, had done some damage. If he needed her blood to prove that he could trust her, Dakota was more than willing.

He pulled back.

"No," she whispered. "Do it. Bite."

"I will not," he told her but he did smile. "You know nothing about me."

"Maybe not," she admitted. "So teach me."

"That I will do," he said as he started to push up her shirt.

Since she was burning from the inside out, the cool feel of his hands eased her some. He unclasped her bra with gentle fingers. Kieran had slowed things down and it was hard for her to remain still. He urged her to lift her shoulders as he pulled off her garments.

Dakota took the opportunity to sit up and grab the bottom of his sweater to yank it over his head. She placed her lips over his heart and peppered kisses across his chest. He wasn't pale, which surprised her some. Even though she'd seen his face and arms, she still had expected the rest of his skin to be white. Maybe she did depend too much on television, movies and vampire legends. Hadn't Kieran already proven so many of those myths wrong? She didn't mind at all letting Kieran teach her anything and everything he wanted.

His skin was flawless, he was just beautiful. She lifted her head to find him watching her. Dakota smiled as she grazed her thumbs over his nipples. Kieran's touch was soft as he cupped her face while lowering his lips to hers once again.

The mixture of ingredients from his drink was still flavorful on his tongue, and Dakota sucked on that appendage, teasing and taunting. He rocked his hips so his erection dragged along her stomach. She reached down and grasped him as best she could through his jeans. With her other hand she began to tug on the button that was keeping her from touching his hard shaft.

Kieran rose to his knees, allowing her better access.

"Take them off," she demanded as she pushed at his waist when she couldn't get his jeans undone.

With a wink, he backed off her to stand at the end of the bed. He ran his hand over his erection and Dakota whimpered. She wanted to be the one that felt him. She moved to go to him, but he took a step away.

"Stay," he told her, pointing his finger at her.

Dakota gave him her sexiest pout. It might have worked since Kieran toed off his shoes before he pulled off his socks. Finally he began to remove his slacks and boxer briefs. She licked her lips as his long cock was revealed.

"Now your turn," he said as he stepped forward. He grabbed ahold of her ankle and tugged her down to the edge of the bed.

He was so strong. That was such a turn on.

She lay against the mattress as he yanked off her boots and quickly worked his way up to getting her naked. The hotel room was warm but she still shivered from the look in his eyes. Kieran appeared to want to devour her and it was intoxicating.

As he wrapped his hand around her calf, Dakota trailed her fingers over her breasts and stomach. Kieran leaned down and licked a path from her knee up her inner thigh.

Dakota tossed her head from side to side, feeling like she was burning up. "Kieran," she whispered.

She wasn't prepared when he brushed his thumb over her clit then moved down to slide his fingers through her slick folds and into her pussy. She moaned, arched and clawed at the blankets at the same time. Two of his long digits pressed inside then withdrew, forcing her to just give in to pleasure.

"Yes," she hissed when his lips covered her clit and he sucked while still fingering her. Before she knew what was happening, she climaxed, shouting for him.

Sitting up, Kieran licked his lips. "You taste wonderful," he told her. He hadn't yet removed his fingers.

"Want you," she whined, reaching for him.

"Yes, now," he said. Kieran lifted her up by her waist and hefted her toward the top of the bed.

Dakota opened her legs and held out her arms. He settled over her so perfectly there was no doubt that was where he belonged. She gripped his face to pull him down so she could kiss him. The taste of her own essence now mixed with the flavors of his drink. She tightened her hold, not wanting him to ever leave, at the same time reaching down and grasping his shaft.

He bucked his hips to push in her hand as their tongues continued to stroke and caress each other. Dakota couldn't hold off anymore. She wrapped her legs around his waist and shimmied closer to get the head of his cock at her entrance.

Kieran thrust hard, and finally, oh God finally, he was inside her.

"Take me," she begged as she ripped her mouth away to breathe.

At first, he withdrew slowly then plunged back with the

same easy movement. Dakota scored her nails down his arms and snarled. She didn't have to be gentle with him as she had her human lovers. If her jaguar came close to the surface, then Kieran could handle it.

To test her theory, she gripped him hard as she rocked against each thrust. Kieran groaned and shuddered as he began to move faster. He slammed inside her, and the bed rocked with them.

Dakota closed her eyes and she urged him on with pleasure-filled sighs. Her breasts were full and achy and her legs shook uncontrollably. She was going to come again.

She pulled him down hard and buried her face in his neck. She nibbled at the exposed flesh, so tender and soft. When the orgasm exploded from her, she bit down, careful not to break skin but marking him the only way she could.

Kieran cried out, then was coming with her. Heat flooded her pussy — it was the first time that she'd felt anything other than coolness from him or his touch.

Shit! Should they have used a condom? She hadn't even thought about that until now as she felt his seed dripping from her pussy.

Dakota collapsed back into the soft mattress. She loved his bed.

Kieran kissed her neck, her cheek then her forehead. He was gentle when he pulled out and lay beside her.

They could talk about condoms and anything else later. All she wanted to do was bask in the afterglow. She curled into his body and sighed deeply when he pulled her close. Good, he was a cuddler. This night just kept getting better and better.

Chapter Three

Dakota yawned as she stretched her arms over her head. Never in her life had she been in such a comfortable bed. There was no confusion about where she was. Her body still felt every ache from the early morning activities.

Just before she'd passed out, Kieran had picked her up and carried her into the bathroom. They'd showered together where he'd washed her body with tender and arousing strokes. Getting clean had been a waste of time since when they'd returned to bed they'd just gotten dirty again.

And again when she'd woken up with him asleep beside her an hour later and had bent over his cock, sucking him awake before she'd straddled his waist and ridden him.

Had it been four or five orgasms? Really she had no clue, but she was feeling the activities pretty damn noticeably now.

She lifted her head and peered around the room. The morning sun crept in through a narrow opening in the curtains. Glancing over to the bedside table, she was shocked to see it was after ten in the morning.

"Damn," she muttered out loud, although she seemed to be completely alone. She breathed deeply, trying to scent Kieran and where he might be. Fuck, she couldn't even do that since she couldn't smell him! She was going to have to get used to Kieran not having a scent and learn to track him another way.

Instead she closed her eyes and concentrated on the sounds in the suite. Nothing, it was silent and still. Where in the hell had he gone? If he'd taken off on her... She sat up again. No, his belongings were still scattered around the room. So he hadn't run away but he wasn't here with her. Dakota pushed off the soft, thick comforters and saw a red rose on the other pillow.

She picked it up and held it to her nose. Sweet and fresh. It was such a romantic gesture that she almost laughed. How could Kieran act so cocky and rude then turn around and leave a rose for her? The man was the master of contradictions.

With a smile and in desperate need of coffee, she climbed out of bed. She didn't immediately see her clothes so she grabbed the sweater Kieran had worn the night before, which was laid over the arm of the chair across from the bed.

She pulled the thick cable-knit sweater over her head before she strode out of the bedroom. The living space in the suite was large and open. The curtains had been tied back and showed an amazing view of the Strip. She'd bet it would be breathtaking at night with all the lights.

Following the faint whiff of coffee, Dakota strolled up to the dining table in front of the windows and lifted a silver-domed lid. A plate of eggs, bacon, sausage, pancakes and fruit lay untouched. She waved her hand over the plate, finding the food still hot, and grinned. She sat then pulled the silver carafe, which she was hoped was full of really good coffee, closer so she could pour a mug.

It couldn't have been that long since Kieran had left if he'd managed to set all this up for her. But why hadn't he woken her? They could have really started the morning off right together.

The coffee tasted just as wonderful as it smelled and she quickly downed half a mug before she refilled it and picked up her fork. The food smelled delicious, and she had worked up an appetite for it the night before.

She needed to check in with her partner to make sure none of the leads from their current case needed her attention right away. She and Dean mainly worked night shifts but there were times when they had to meet with witnesses or trail a suspect during the day.

Of course that meant she needed to find her clothes and purse. That could wait until she'd eaten breakfast, though. The pancakes were fluffy and the bacon crispy. She'd never stayed in this hotel before but now she knew what she'd been missing. How nice it would be to just order up whatever you wanted, whenever you wanted.

In the past she'd met other agents who rented out hotels or motels on a weekly basis but she couldn't justify spending so much money. Not that she didn't have enough. The Organization paid well but working for them didn't really give her a lot of time for spending any of it. Maybe this was how Kieran always lived.

It was obvious that he liked his comforts. The extra blankets and pillows. The sweater she had borrowed and the thick jacket he'd had on in the alley. Maybe no one else had noticed but it was obvious to Dakota that Kieran liked soft and comfortable things. And she knew how to work with that.

Dakota finished her breakfast and drained her coffee then poured one more cup. She stood with her mug in her hand and ambled around, just looking. It appeared that Kieran was here to stay for a little while. He'd unpacked and there were little items all over the hotel room. She spotted a hanger with plastic wrap on the back of the couch and strode over.

Through the cover her slacks were visible. She set her coffee down on a table close by and lifted up the dry cleaning. What the hell time had Kieran gotten up?

Not that she could complain. Fresh clothes to change into, good food with better coffee. The only thing she could complain about was the fact that he was nowhere to be seen.

With a sigh, she carried her clothing as she walked to the shower. Might as well prepare for the day. Hopefully Kieran would be back before she left.

* * * *

Kieran remained hidden behind a concrete barrier as Dakota and Dean left the apartment they'd spent the last twenty minutes inside. He wasn't sure what case they were working or why they kept stopping to talk to people, and he really didn't care. He was bored.

God, was this what other agents did?

He, Remy and Angel usually heard about an area where trouble was and staked it out. When they witnessed anyone attempting to hurt an innocent or cause problems, they stepped in and took care of things. Although they couldn't kill anyone anymore, which sort of bummed him out.

He'd also been assigned to protection details a lot lately.

But never had he had to run down leads or investigate. That was what Angel and Remy did before they called him in. Maybe he should give more credit to his partners because this sucked.

He straddled his bike and waited until Dakota and Dean were driving away before he revved the engine and followed at a discreet distance. There had to be some way to add adventure to the night. His entire plan of following them instead of the other way around was backfiring on him.

When Dean drove the dark SUV toward his hotel, Kieran grew excited. As Dakota had slept, Kieran had used his time wisely and added to the information he was collecting on Caspar's nephew, Dean. He now knew where Dean lived, worked out, shopped and ate lunch. Kieran had followed him for several hours before Dakota had joined him.

They'd met at a small diner close to the Air Force base. When he'd seen Dakota again after leaving her cuddled up in his bed, Kieran had felt an intense hunger come over him.

Even though he shouldn't have to feed yet, Kieran's fangs had dropped down and the thirst had almost overpowered all common sense. For the first time in years he'd been afraid. Scared that he could have lost control and hurt someone.

It'd only lasted for a few minutes, less than five, before

the craving had passed.

By that time Dakota had been sitting across from Dean as they'd eaten lunch and she was safe. Kieran had already decided that he'd feed before he went back to his hotel for the night. Now, hours later, Dean was leading him back in that direction.

Instead of pulling around to the casino entrance, Dean drove through the lot and into the employee parking garage. Kieran parked his motorcycle in one of the spots used by the valets in the open hotel spaces instead of following the SUV. He shut down before he climbed off and peered toward the parking lot where Dean's vehicle had disappeared. He attached his helmet to the side of his bike before he used his speed to reach the same area without anyone noticing him.

The dark SUV had pulled to a stop in front of the elevators and sat idling. Dakota and Dean were still inside. What were they doing?

The elevator opened—Kieran couldn't see it, but heard the metal grinding and the squeak of the doors. He crawled between vehicles until he came out of the other side. From this view, he could see a man standing outside Dean's window talking to him. The guy looked vaguely familiar but Kieran couldn't place him. Kieran could only see the back and a slight side of his face every so often.

He closed his eyes and opened all his senses.

"Not been in his room all day," the stranger said. "I checked with the housekeeper who cleaned this morning and there's no sign of him."

Dean cursed, causing Kieran to smile.

So they were looking for him and had guys inside the hotel. Smart. He just needed the guy to turn around.

"He'll come back," Dean said. "Hell, I wouldn't be surprised if he turned the tables and is watching us."

Dakota snorted.

"What?" Dean asked while the hotel staffer leaned into the open window.

"He's been following us all day on a motorcycle," Dakota answered. "Last I saw him, he pulled off when we pulled into this parking garage."

"What?" Dean's voice rose.

The hotel staffer laughed as he finally turned around. The man who'd brought him his dinner — that was why he looked familiar. Damn, Dean and Dakota were good.

He hadn't expected Dakota to spot him. The fact that she had? Wow, that was fucking hot. She kept surprising him. There was no way that she had picked up his scent since he didn't have one. Most shifters used their noses to hunt and track but with him, Dakota didn't have that option.

So how in the hell had she seen him?

"Fuck," Dean cursed then started to look around.

Kieran had the urge to step out and wave. *Hell, why not.* He stepped out from behind a blue van. The hotel staffer saw him first and smacked the side of the SUV.

Dean stuck his head out of the window and frowned at him. Kieran sent him a wink before he backed away and sped out of the parking garage. It was time to take care of personal business.

They knew he would return to his hotel and he expected it would be Dakota who would be checking on him.

He had something to look forward to then.

When he reached his bike, he grabbed up his helmet and put it on. He threw his leg over the seat before he started up the engine. He'd picked up the smaller bike to stalk the Organization agents for the night.

Of course eventually the owner would wonder where it was so he had to ditch it after he was finished for the night. Since he'd stolen it from someone who'd done the same Kieran hadn't felt bad one bit.

He drove out of the hotel lot and raced toward the same part of town he'd been in the previous night. If there was trouble to be found, no doubt that was the area he needed to be in. It had worked for him before.

After ten minutes, Kieran pulled into a space at a closed

medical clinic. He took a rag from his back pocket and started to wipe down the bike. Even though he'd worn gloves, it was important to be careful. One of the first lessons Caspar had taught him was to never leave a trace of himself behind.

Once he was sure that he'd left no evidence, Kieran simply walked away.

The cops would find the bike and get it to its rightful owner. He had actually helped the guy out since the punk who'd stolen it in the first place would have probably destroyed it.

As Kieran strolled along the streets, he kept all of his senses open. Normally he would never feed off a human but he couldn't take the chance of losing control around Dakota. It was a risk he was taking tonight but he had no other choice.

At first when he'd needed to feed, Kieran would pay someone off the street a ridiculous amount so they would keep their mouths shut. It had helped someone in need while keeping himself safe. But considering every time he bit someone they got sick, he always felt bad about causing that for someone who just needed money. If he was desperate he'd take that avenue but Kieran had found other ways to hunt. He just had to wait until someone approached him without good intentions and let that decide for him.

The night was cool so he was glad of his leather jacket. Still, it would be easier to look like a victim if he didn't have it. As he considered stashing it somewhere, the sound of footsteps reached him.

Kieran stumbled a little while waving his arms around. The drunken ploy usually worked like a charm.

He heard laughing and knew he'd scored. There was a group of four men headed toward him on the opposite side of the street. As soon as they spotted him, Kieran ran himself into the building to his right. He stopped, cursed, before he kicked at it.

"Look at that guy."

"Outta my way," Kieran slurred at the wall.

"Let's roll him," someone said. "And I want that jacket."

Kieran whirled around, making sure he tipped to the side. He hit the ground hard and groaned.

"Hurry." The harsh whisper was close.

"Hey, buddy, let us help you."

Kieran glanced up into the dark eyes of a man who couldn't have been more than twenty.

"Hi." Kieran waved.

"How about a hand?" The young guy reached down from him.

"Thanks!" Kieran said then laughed. "How'd I get down here?" Kieran grabbed at the offered hand but the guy moved quickly and punched him.

That did it. This was the one who he would feed from. No one deserved to be sucker-punched. No longer needing the ruse, Kieran leaped to his feet and grabbed his opponent by the neck. Kieran slammed the guy face first into the building.

One of the others shouted then struck out at him. Kieran kicked him in the knee, taking him down before he slammed his fist into the thug's face, knocking him out cold. The remaining two came at Kieran at the same time. Smart, but he easily took care of them.

"Now," he said out loud to no one since all four men were unconscious. "My turn."

He walked over to the first guy and hefted him up to his feet so he could shove him against the brick. Kieran grabbed the guy's wrist and bit down.

If the thug were awake, he'd feel the sting of his teeth. Kieran took a deep drink and let the blood flow through him. The consuming of blood warmed his cool body. For a few minutes he didn't feel the normal chill that was always with him.

One of the reasons that Kieran fed so rarely was so he didn't get used to the feeling. A Day Walker could start to crave the warmth and would take too much blood and start killing. There was no need for death. A few sips was all it took to reenergize him and temporarily ease the hunger.

Kieran ripped his mouth away from the wrist in his hold and took a deep breath. Once the guy woke up, he would become sick. The worst symptoms would be stomach cramps and vomiting.

There was a poison in his body that destroyed the good blood cells and tainted them. When he drank he replenished the good blood and slowed down the poison. When his fangs pierced someone's flesh, the poison entered into his source in a trace amount. Humans normally were sick for a couple of hours. Shifters, like Remy, got a headache and less severe symptoms.

When not on a case, Remy always volunteered to feed him and Angel but Kieran didn't want his friend to think they were using him so he tried to get his blood the way he'd done tonight.

He allowed the thug to slide down the wall and took a step back. The others were still out also so he left them where they'd fallen. If anything else happened to them it wasn't really his fault. They'd attacked him after all.

Kieran turned and sauntered back down the block. He'd wait until he got to a crowded part of the city then would hail a cab to the hotel. As he strolled he kept his ear tuned to hear for any trouble. It was still early so he had plenty of time before he had to get back to the hotel. Hopefully Dakota would already be there waiting for him.

It was a quiet night, though, and he got all the way to downtown without coming across anyone. At a well-lit corner he spotted a hotel with a taxi line. Kieran jogged across the street and jumped into the first one available.

He gave the name of his hotel and sat back. The lights had turned on all over the city and it was bright and loud. The closer they got to Strip, the lower Kieran sank down. He really hated being surrounded by all these strangers.

The large billboard in front of his hotel came into view and he relaxed. Almost home, well his temporary home, where he could shower and put on some comfortable clothes. The warmth had already left him and he just wanted a night in. Maybe he could even convince Dakota to use the Jacuzzi tub with him.

Kieran pulled out his wallet and paid the taxi driver with a good tip before he pushed the door open. One of the hotel attendants ran over and hovered at the side of the cab.

"Checking in, sir?" he asked. "Can I get your luggage?"

"I'm already in twelve-oh-three," he told the young man as he walked away. "But thank you."

"If you need anything, just let me know," the kid called out.

Kieran nodded. He really was enjoying his stay here, although he would have to keep an eye out for more of the Organization's spies. If Caspar had asked Dean to keep watch over him, it might not be through the official channels. That would work better for Kieran. He could continue to mess with Dean. Kieran could no doubt think of some really fun tricks to play on him. He did hope that he could keep Dakota out of things even if he had challenged her the night before.

He didn't want to go up against Dakota no matter what he'd told her. For the first time since he'd been rescued, he wanted to get to know a shifter better on an intimate level. It was more than that, though — he didn't think of her as a shifter first. If she were human, he wouldn't even be thinking twice about being with her. He'd have probably hit on her in the alley where they met. So he was going to enjoy what time he had left.

Two weeks with her, then he would have to leave and return to the shadows. He worked in the dark where he was most comfortable. As much as he looked forward to the next couple of weeks they would have to end.

He swiped his key card in the elevator to take him to his floor. The dark elegance in the lift was classy and comfortable. It had been the right decision to move into here. He was sort of glad that Dean had forced his hand.

Kieran stepped out onto his floor and strolled to his door. It had been much more fun the night before when he'd been carrying Dakota in his arms. Just thinking about that had him speeding up and rushing to get inside. He ran his card through the reader before he pushed the door open.

The quietness of the suite was a disappointment. He had no doubt that if Dakota wanted in his room, she'd have found a way. The fact that she hadn't crushed Kieran and he had to push away the rare feeling of loneliness. He liked being on his own and he didn't need anyone around to make him feel important. He snorted, knowing he was lying to himself.

He closed the door behind him and tossed the card onto the table. Kieran pulled off his jacket and threw it on the back of the couch before he strolled into the bedroom. He undressed and laid his clothes on the chair then walked toward the bathroom.

The sweater he'd worn the night before was lying on the made-up bed. Kieran brought it to his nose and breathed in the sweet scent of Dakota. She had actually worn his clothing. Oh hell, that was sexy.

"Dakota," he whispered as he dragged the sweater down his neck, then over his chest and stomach, before he rubbed his cock. He'd grown hard the minute he'd picked up her scent.

Her spicy, stimulating smell was all around him and now on his body. He wrapped the fabric around his erection and stroked himself. *Fuck, that's good.* Kieran dropped down on the bed and laid himself out. He picked up the sleeve with his free hand and placed it over his nose before he reached down and cupped his balls.

Jacking himself off and pulling on his balls, Kieran closed his eyes and thought about Dakota. He imagined it was Dakota's smaller hand instead of his stroking up and down his cock. Kieran braced his feet on the mattress and lifted his knees to thrust his erection through his fingers.

Yes, yes, just like that. He pumped his hips wildly until he was coming all over his sweater. Out of breath, he flopped back on the bed and sprawled out. He was sated and would have really liked to burrow into the blankets and take a nap but he wanted a shower and food first.

With a groan, he pulled himself off the mattress. He picked up the room-service menu and browsed it. He could go down to one of the nine restaurants, or even some of the clubs that served food, but Kieran had had his fill of people for the day.

Instead he would relax in his suite. A lighter meal than he'd had the night before sounded good. He lifted the hotel phone receiver and pressed the button that looked like a fork and knife for room service. His call was answered right away.

"Good evening, Mr. Nichols."

"I'd like to order some room service?" he said.

"Yes, sir, can we get dinner prepared for you, Mr. Nichols?" the hotel staffer asked.

He wondered if it was the same man as the night before. The one that had been talking to Dean and Dakota earlier. Oh well, that didn't really matter. "Yes, I'd like to order the wood-grilled chicken, a loaded baked potato, whatever fresh vegetables you have today and some rolls."

"Very good, sir, how about dessert or drinks?"

"A pot of coffee and water would be great," Kieran confirmed.

"We'll have your order up to you shortly, sir. Please let us know if you need anything else and have a good night."

"Thank you, you too," Kieran replied. He hung up, shaking his head. He really needed to not get used to this treatment. Since he was still holding his sweater—which needed to be cleaned—he strolled to the bathroom and grabbed the laundry service bag off the back door. He stuffed his sweater inside before he stepped over to the shower. He turned on the faucets then glanced around the space.

It appeared Dakota had made herself at home in there too.

A small, hotel-provided toothbrush sat in a cup next to his own. Her hairbrush was also mixed in with his belongings. Surely she'd be coming back.

Disgusted with himself for wondering and for pining over her again, he hopped into the shower and let the hot water cascade over his head. Two weeks, that was how long he had left in the city. He couldn't get any more attached to her than he could to the hotel services. In just a short couple of weeks he'd be back on the road with Remy and Angel. Even if he managed to come back to Vegas, it could be months or a year before that might happen.

No, he couldn't make Dakota or himself any promises.

Kieran picked up his body wash and poured some into his hand. It might not be easy but he had to stick with his decision. Yes, he would spend time with Dakota but he would have to back off slightly too. He never fell for a woman, knew he wouldn't be around anywhere long. Dakota was no different from any other women he'd slept with.

And still he knew he was lying.

He scrubbed his body roughly, hoping that the pain might take his mind away from his thoughts. He showered quickly, looking forward to relaxing with dinner.

A new towel hung next to the shower on the warmer. No matter what, he was getting a towel warmer for his place. That was a luxury he could afford and wanted. Remy would probably give him a hard time but no more so than how Kieran teased Remy about the pile of blankets that he kept on the floor for when he wanted to have puppy piles. And those were his words not Kieran's.

After drying off his body, Kieran dropped the towel onto the tub and walked naked back into the bedroom. In the dresser he found a soft pair of gray sweats and a faded white T-shirt. He pulled them on before going barefoot into the main room. He was about to sit when a knock came at the door. His food was a little earlier than he'd expected but that was good since he was hungry.

Out of habit he glanced through the peephole but didn't find the hotel attendant. Suspicious, he angled his body to the right of the door. He unlocked and opened it slowly.

The man was at least six-two with neatly styled black hair and he wore an expensive looking black suit.

"Yes?" Kieran asked.

"Blake Nichols, or should I say Kieran Smith?" The voice was smooth and polite.

"Who's asking?" Kieran questioned. He gripped the door tightly but prepared himself in case he needed to use his hands.

"My name is Alex Hamilton and I'm the head of security here."

"I have no need for security and I haven't done anything, so what do you want?" Kieran asked. He stood straight and crossed his arms over his chest, showing off his muscles.

The guy looked up and that was when Kieran noticed his unusual blue eyes and the fact that he didn't have a scent. In surprise, Kieran took a step back.

Another Day Walker? It was rare for Kieran to ever come across one like himself. "What do you want?"

"Just a word," Alex said with a nod. "In private if you don't mind."

Kieran did mind but he was also curious. He pushed the door wider and motioned Alex inside. Kieran knew he was opening himself up for serious trouble.

Chapter Four

Kieran let Alex walk past him into the living room as he watched his every move. A Day Walker that worked security for the hotel? How had Kieran not known about him? Did Caspar or the Organization know of his existence? Questions flooded him but he was too stubborn to ask.

"Can we sit for a minute?" Alex asked.

"Sure." Kieran nodded. He waited until Alex sat on the couch before he dropped onto the leather chair across from him. Once he was seated, Kieran looked Alex over.

It was obvious that Alex had money but the power that radiated off him was unexpected. Most Walkers he'd met through his job were weak and dirty from their fight with craving blood. Kieran didn't expect any conversation with Alex to go well. He'd been caught using his fake identification and there was no good reason for security to be in his suite. Still, he didn't kick Alex out as he really was curious about the Walker. In his experience other Day Walkers struggled to live in the modern world. If Kieran and his partners came across one, it was because they were killing or bringing attention to themselves.

"I meant to make it by last night but I got caught up in work," Alex said. "I wanted to welcome you."

"Welcome me?" he repeated. "Why?"

"There's not very many of us. The few I've met over the years didn't deserve the gift we have. It wasn't until I began working here that I found out how well my life could truly be," Alex said.

"And how did you come to this realization?" Kieran asked, honestly curious.

"This hotel and the entire line of casinos is owned by one of us," Alex told him.

"Who?" Could that be right? What else didn't Kieran know about his people and where and how they lived? He'd always felt so alone. Well, until Caspar had taken him in and introduced him to Angel. If what Alex was saying was indeed true, he could learn so much.

But it could also be a trap. There had to be a reason he didn't know about the Day Walkers in town. If they were criminals, it would be Kieran's job to take them down.

"I'm sure with your resources you can find out whatever you want about the owner," Alex said. "However, Jackson would like to meet you later this week if you agree. He's out of the country at the moment but should return by late Wednesday evening."

Kieran found himself nodding even though he hadn't actually made up his mind.

"In the meantime your room and any charges you have or may rack up are on us. We'd like to make sure you enjoy your stay," Alex said.

Now Kieran was really suspicious. "I can't accept that."

"We'll call it evens in case we have any trouble here and need your assistance. We have a good working relationship with your Organization and hope you'll help if it's needed."

So his company did know about them. That relieved him a little. Still... "Why haven't I ever heard about you or this owner?" he asked, remaining blunt. Knowledge was his business and he really didn't like that this man had caught him off guard.

"Our agreement with your Organization is that we remain hidden and cause no trouble. They leave us to our business and don't out us to anyone else. We are in the profession of secrets. Yours to protect and ours to remain unknown. We knew the minute you got to town."

Kieran sat forward in his chair. "Someone called you?" If Caspar had given Kieran more babysitters, then he was really going to lose his mind, so to speak.

"No," Alex said quickly. "We have people all over the city. They know how to recognize our kind. Before you arrived here yesterday, we didn't know anything about you other than that you were here on vacation. But when you changed hotels, I grew concerned. We've had problems in the past with Walkers coming in and thinking they could do whatever they wanted."

Kieran could see why that would be a problem. He also wanted to know who'd spotted him and how. He held off asking, not wanting to give away his inability to do the same.

"So after you checked in I did some digging around," Alex said.

He knew that any official information found would be light on info.

"When I couldn't find much, I phoned my contact within the Organization. Alex verified Kieran's earlier thought. "All I could get was that you are on the job. And that was good enough for me."

"Okay," Kieran said. "So what exactly do you want from me?"

"Like I said, hopefully nothing." Alex braced his elbows on his knees. "In the last six months, we've seen more and more supernatural types in town. It's kept my employees busy and we're concerned that someone might be up to something. If there's trouble, we'd like to be able to call on you. We'll even go through official channels but having you here actually works out well for us."

"So you don't only run security for the hotel but the entire city?" Kieran asked. That was what the cops, Coalition and Organization were for. If Alex and his people were vigilantes, Kieran had to look into it.

"No." Alex shook his head then nodded. "Or maybe. Jackson was the first of our kind that settled in the city. He looks at this as his responsibility and he isn't going to let trouble put any of us in danger. Part of my job is to ensure that."

Kieran really wanted to meet this Jackson…after he'd looked a little more into the entire operation in Vegas. "How many of us are there in the city?"

"A dozen." Alex shrugged. "More or less as people travel. But living here, under the radar, and who we keep tabs on? Twelve."

"Okay," Kieran said. "I want to talk to my people, although while I'm doing that, I'll remain open to offering my services if needed."

Alex smiled. "I appreciate that." He stood, so Kieran rose as well. "You know you're being watched, right?"

Kieran laughed. "Very much so. I'm having fun with it. It's personal and I'm not in any danger."

"Okay." Alex held out his hand. "If you need any help, just let me know. Been a while since I've had any fun."

For some unknown reason Kieran liked the man in front of him. He felt comfortable, and although he wanted to be wary, he just couldn't manage it. He grinned back at Alex. "We might be able to work something up."

"That'd be great." They shook before Alex headed toward the door. "If you'd like to get a drink sometime, give me a call. I imagine you'll have more questions after you've done some poking around on us."

Kieran figured the same.

"I'll be happy to tell you what I can." Alex handed him a card. "My office and personal numbers."

"Thanks." Kieran accepted the card.

Alex turned to open the door and stepped out. Kieran stood in the doorway as Alex strolled down to the elevator. This was an interesting turn of events. What had happened to his boring vacation? He hadn't planned on the Organization agents following him or this new twist.

Crap! Remy was headed to him any day. He would prefer to keep his friend away from these guys. If what Alex had said was true, that they tracked every supernatural person who came into their city, the minute Remy arrived they would know.

He could call his friend off. Remy wouldn't be happy but he'd deal with it. Although Kieran needed his bribe for Lettie even more now that he had additional work for her to do.

Before he could close the door, he heard the elevator ding and the doors open. He could smell the rich bold aroma of coffee. His dinner.

Alex entered the lift as the hotel staffer exited it. They nodded at each other in a familiar fashion. Kieran narrowed his eyes as he watched the man who wheeled his food in his direction. He picked up the scent of berries and grass. He took a deep breath. *Shifter, bear.* He jerked back in surprise.

"Good evening, sir," the staffer said. "I hope you weren't waiting long."

"No," Kieran said. "I was letting my guest out."

"Should I bring the cart in?"

Kieran stepped out of the way. "If you could place it on the table, please."

"Sure."

As the young man busied himself with setting out Kieran's meal, Kieran watched him closely. The bear shifter's heart rate was calm and steady. He didn't smell nervous or afraid. Just a normal guy doing his job? Kieran wasn't so sure. He was pretty certain Alex was showing him that the hotel was full of supernatural people.

It's what he would do.

"Do you need anything else?"

"That should be it," Kieran said as he accepted the leather case to sign. Again he added a generous tip before he handed it back over. It wasn't his money he was spending anymore.

"Just call if you need anything else, sir."

He nodded then closed and locked his door. His stomach growled as he strode over to the table. He started to make a mental list. He needed to call Lettie and Remy, and depending on what Lettie told him, maybe Caspar. As much as he hated reports, there was a good chance he'd be spending the rest of his night researching the city and occupants.

Alex had stated that he had a contact within the Organization. He wanted to find out who that was. If it was Dean or Dakota, that would simplify things for him. Since he wasn't normally that lucky, he suspected that it wouldn't be that easy. It would give him the opportunity, though, to see who else worked for his company in Vegas.

Maybe tomorrow he would stake out their building. There had to be somewhere that they worked out of.

If he could find a way inside, he might really have some amusement. Caspar would probably be pissed if Kieran did so, which made him want to break in even more. He did need to pay his boss back for putting Dean on him. Hell, he might be able to get into Dean's office and screw with both Caspar and his nephew. Excited now, Kieran started on his dinner.

He savored every delicious bite of his meal as he worked out what he wanted to do. First he had to check his emails for what he'd asked Lettie for the night before. She'd had almost twenty-four hours so he had no doubt Lettie would have come through for him by now. He'd also have to send her the new names to look into while he worked on going through case files there in Vegas.

Kieran finished his first mug of coffee then poured another. After he'd eaten the last couple of bites of dinner, he sat back in his chair and groaned. That had been so damn tasty. If the hotel was footing the bill, maybe he should think about eating lunch there also?

No, he wouldn't take advantage. They might ask him for his help or might not. If not, he'd pay for his expenses but if there was any need for him to get involved, he'd allow them to pay.

He wasn't sure how he felt about this new development in his life. Twelve Day Walkers, fourteen if he included himself and Alex. Alex had said that he kept in contact with them, so did they work within the hotels or just live in the area?

His cell phone rang and he glanced around. Ah, bedroom, where he'd undressed. Kieran pushed back from the table and strolled through the living area. His pants were still on the chair he'd left them on. Kieran picked them up and dug in the pocket until he pulled out his cell.

"Hey," he greeted after he'd swept his finger over the screen to answer.

"I'm a day away," Remy told him. "I should be in late tomorrow night. What hotel should I check into?"

Well, shit. Kieran didn't want his partner at his hotel or anywhere near Alex until he knew what was going on. Maybe not even then. "Ugh."

Remy laughed. "I'm not feeling the love. What's going on?"

Remy should know what was going on. He'd want to help, but Kieran would deal with that later. "I don't want to get into it over the phone. But can you trust me?"

All trace of amusement left Remy's voice. "Of course."

"Grab a hotel on the strip but don't use the Graham chain," Kieran told him.

"No problem," Remy agreed. "I'll text you my hotel and room number. You want to meet me there when I get in?"

"Yeah," Kieran agreed. That would give him enough time to do his research, stalk around and come up with a plan.

"Watch your back," Remy said.

"Will do," Kieran promised before he hung up. Since he had his pants in his hand he gathered up the rest of his clothing and added them into the same laundry bag he'd shoved his sweater in earlier. He glanced at the bed — it was mussed up a little but not too bad. And he appreciated that housekeeping had added the same amount of blankets and pillows he'd had on it the night before.

He had work to do and strode into the living area. Kieran went directly to the curtains that hid the large windows. He pulled them open, giving him an astonishing view of the Strip. There were hundreds of people on the streets right now, and any one of them could be a Walker. *Okay, enough stalling.* He rubbed his hands together. Research was needed, and as much as he hated it, if he wanted answers, the job had to get done. He grabbed his laptop from the table where he'd left it the night before and took it to the desk that sat right next to the window. At least he'd have the view to appreciate as he sorted through files.

Humming, he opened the computer lid and powered it on before he strolled back over to the table and poured himself a fresh cup of coffee. He carried it with him to the desk and sat. Kieran logged on and waited. He had to connect to the Internet, glad he'd ordered the extra amenity even if it was an additional fee. Then he logged into his secure server so his movements couldn't be followed.

After he was as protected as possible, he opened his emails. As expected there were two emails from Lettie. The subject lines were the names that she'd researched for him. He was surprised to see one from his boss as well.

Kieran opened Caspar's first. He grinned as he read. It was the basic checking-in talk and telling Kieran to behave himself. There was no chance in hell he'd be doing that. But the email did tell him that Dean hadn't spoken to Caspar yet.

He closed the email without responding. Let Caspar wonder what he was up to. Next, he hovered the mouse icon over the email with Dakota's name in the subject line. Did he want to go there? When he'd first asked Lettie to look into her, it had been before they'd slept together. Now it seemed…creepy. He already knew her, didn't he?

Earlier he'd admitted to himself that he didn't see Dakota as a shifter that was out to hurt him. There was a big part of him that wanted to keep that fantasy alive. What if he found something that changed his feelings about her? Maybe her family, or other shifters she knew, had captured or tortured Walkers like those who'd taken him. He wouldn't be able to stand it.

Cowardly maybe, but Kieran chose the email for Dean

first.

There was no message, just an attachment that he double clicked open. A picture of a younger Dean was the first thing he saw. He was a good-looking kid who'd grown into a handsome man. He'd resembled Caspar more when he'd been younger. They shared the same square chin and high cheekbones. It was hard to hate the guy when he reminded Kieran so much of a man he cared for.

He scrolled down past the picture. Dean had attended the Organization's boarding school in California. So Angel and Remy probably wouldn't know him. They'd both gone to school on the east coast. Dean had been a good student who'd aced all his classes, especially math and science. Kieran read about all of Dean's accomplishments and was impressed. If he'd been in charge, he would have put Dean in a lab or as a technician. He would thrive investigating, just like Lettie. Maybe Dean was good in the field but he had a feeling that it was his last name that had decided his position.

Vaguely, he wondered how Dean felt about that.

According to the file, Dean had been partnered with Dakota for three years. A long partnership that had benefited the city of Las Vegas. There was little on his personal affairs in the file but that was to be expected. The juicy stuff would be harder to find, but Kieran was a determined man.

He minimized this email and pulled up the program that gave him access to the Organization's files. He typed in a request for cases in the Las Vegas area for the last six months.

Jesus! Over four hundred open, closed and current cases. How did the agents there get anything done? To narrow down the numbers, he typed in Dean's name. That was a little more manageable. Still just shy of one hundred. He picked the newest and opened it. He'd work his way back. If he didn't get a good idea of how Dean and Dakota worked after reading through these, he didn't know how he would.

* * * *

It was almost ten at night but no one had seen Kieran leave his suite, so Dakota hoped he was still in for the night. After she and Dean had left the hotel earlier, they'd been called in to assist some of the other agents.

A group of shifters had decided to try their hand at breaking and entering. They'd used brute force instead of finesse and that was what had got them busted. It wasn't hard to follow their scents to where they'd crashed.

But that had made her later than she'd wanted.

She knocked softly on Kieran's hotel door so as not to disturb the occupants in the rooms around him. Dakota leaned closer to the door and could hear sounds. She moved from foot to foot as she waited.

When he opened the door, her breath caught. Kieran wore only a pair of sweats and a T-shirt. She hadn't seen him dressed down before and she liked it. Almost as much as when he was naked. He looked good in his street clothes but now? He actually took her breath away. His hair was ruffled like he'd been running his fingers through it. To see him so laid-back and in comfort made her feel like she was seeing a side of him very few did.

Without a word, he opened the door the rest of the way. She stepped in and picked up the smell of coffee, food and wine? It had to have been a better meal than what she and Dean had picked up on the fly. Dean loved fast food, and while Dakota tried her best to shovel some of the same crap down, she always felt slightly nauseous after.

Kieran closed the door and with a hand to her lower back, led her into the living space of the suite. The suite looked even more lived in than it had the night before. The room wasn't as neat as when she'd left earlier but still tidier than her own place. She wondered if he was always neat or if it was just because he was in a hotel room.

"Would you like a drink?" he asked as he strolled to the table ahead of her. "I had a bottle brought up."

"Yes, please," she replied as she shrugged off her coat and placed it over Kieran's on the back of the couch.

Kieran poured her a glass of a dark red liquid then strolled toward her. "I'd wondered if I would see you tonight."

She accepted the glass as she nodded. "I got caught up in work." She glanced around and saw that he'd been working on something himself at the desk. His laptop was open and he had a notebook sitting next to it. If he was on vacation, was that for business or pleasure?

He followed her gaze. "Research."

When he didn't elaborate, she shrugged it off. She knew that Kieran was still wary of her. She wished she knew what his problem with shifters was so she would be able to make him more comfortable.

She could call Caspar or have Dean do it but then she'd have to admit that her interest was personal. Not that she was ashamed of it, but Dakota had a feeling that Caspar wouldn't want anyone to know about her and Kieran.

She'd even thought about calling up his file but that felt like a breach of trust. All she could do was hope that eventually he would be comfortable enough to share his past with her. Her only worry was that something would come between them before he fully trusted her. Dakota knew she would fight for him but if he was the one pushing her away, she wasn't certain she would succeed. It was very obvious that he was damn stubborn. She glanced over at him and saw him watching her. Dakota smiled before she took a sip of her wine.

"Have you eaten?" he asked.

"We grabbed something at the drive-through earlier," she told him. "After you stopped following us."

Kieran laughed. "You have to tell me how you spotted me."

"It was easy," she said while strolling to the window to look down at her city. "Yours is the best ass I've ever seen. I'd know it anywhere."

She saw him approach in the reflection in the windows.

Kieran placed his hand on her shoulder before he leaned into her. Holding her glass in her right hand, she reached back to grasp the back of his leg to hold him close.

"I thought I was sneakier than that," he said.

Dakota sipped more of the smooth liquid. It had a good, bold flavor that she appreciated. She leaned more toward hard liquor or beer but this was nice. Especially with Kieran pressed up against her as she watched the lights twinkle below. "You probably are but since you were on my mind, it most likely made it easier."

"On your mind?" he asked. He brought his arms around her to place his hands over her stomach.

She allowed herself to rest her weight against him while continuing to drink. "You know you were," she said. It was easier to speak her mind not having to look at him. "I was impressed this morning."

"I hope you were impressed last night, in the middle of the night *and* this morning," he teased.

Dakota laughed. "Yeah, yeah, I was but I was talking about my clothes and breakfast."

He sighed, and she started to turn around but he tightened his hold. Maybe this was less demanding for him too, not having to face her as they spoke. "I didn't want you to feel like… Just…even though I was gone this morning, I enjoyed our time together and hoped you'd be back."

She smiled at his confession so she gave him one of her own. "There was no way I wasn't coming back, whether you wanted me to or not."

"Good," he whispered before he brushed his lips over the side of her neck. "I'd hate to have to track you down."

"And you would, wouldn't you?" she asked.

"I believe I proved that today," he said.

"True," she agreed. "But I have a feeling that was more professional than to chase after me."

He brushed his cheek over the top of her head. "Okay, but I behaved myself because you were in the vehicle."

Dakota laughed. "Well, I appreciate that. So I guess

you're not going to lump me in the same bracket with Dean anymore? I'm safe from what other people told us could be very imaginable payback?"

"You were safe the minute I walked into the bar last night and saw you," he confessed. "Your partner is not."

"He's just doing what his uncle's asked," Dakota pointed out.

Kieran tsked her. "Nope. You can't take sides or I won't be able to guarantee your safety."

"Safety?" she asked. "I really like my partner and don't want to break in a new one. Do not kill him."

He sighed. "Fine, I won't kill him."

If Kieran didn't sound so serious, she would be amused. As it was she was a little frightened for what Dean had gotten himself into. "You promise?" she pressed.

"Yes," he replied. He skimmed his hands up to cup her breasts and began to knead. That was one way to change the subject.

Dakota dropped her head back against his solid chest and arched her back so that she was pressing into his touch. Her nipples hardened as her breath sped up. The electric current that she'd felt the night before was still there, but now instead of being surprised she just enjoyed it.

"Kieran," she murmured. "We really should talk."

He groaned and the vibration against her back tickled some. "I just agreed not to kill your partner. I also promise not to maim him or take him out of duty. There, nothing else to talk about!" He ended with scraping his teeth on her ear.

Dakota moaned and had to fight herself from giving in. "That is not what I meant. We can't just jump straight into bed this time."

"Why not?" he asked.

She frowned and turned around. "Seriously?" Didn't he wonder where this was going between the two of them?

"What?" he asked as he ran his hand through his hair. It surprised her when he took a step back from her. Like he hadn't just been seconds from dragging her off to bed or taking her right there on the floor.

"How do you do that?" she asked before she downed the rest of her wine. She stalked over to the table before she picked up the bottle, refilling her glass.

"What are you talking about?" He sounded frustrated, and since he was showing some sort of emotion, she relaxed some. If he argued and fought, then he was invested.

"How do you turn it off and on like that?" she asked. "Is it because I'm a shifter?"

"Don't." He pointed his finger. "I'm trying not to think about the fact that you're a shifter."

Bottle in one hand and glass in the other Dakota froze. "You want to repeat that?" she asked in warning.

Kieran strode across the living area then back to her. "I didn't mean it that way," he finally said after a few tense moments.

"I think you did," she said. Dakota set the wine and glass down. Why did that hurt so much? She barely knew Kieran but hadn't she been thinking long term? Just earlier she'd been prepared to fight for him but if he couldn't ever accept her jaguar, what could she do? She was part shifter — that was just who and what she was. "I've been telling myself that I could convince you that I'm not like whoever hurt you in the past. You just need time to see me as a person first."

"I do," he told her.

They were only about ten feet away from each other but it felt like so much more. "No," she said. "You're lying to yourself. Because you don't see me as a person first — you only see me as a person. You're ignoring the biggest part of me."

"Being a shifter isn't the biggest part of you," he argued.

"Yes, it is," she said. "It's my work, my friends and family, and what I am on the inside. I love my jaguar. I love to shift. And I won't stop even for you."

"I'm not asking you to," Kieran said.

"Not yet," she said, her heart breaking a little. "Eventually you'd see me shift. And that would be the reminder that sends you running."

"I don't run," he told her.

Dakota pressed her lips together. She stared at him, having to fight herself from going to him. Kieran solved the problem by marching straight to her and pulling her into his arms. He kissed her, hard and deep.

She moaned into his mouth as she wrapped her arms around his neck. Yes, it was wrong and she doubted he'd ever accept her shifter part but if this was the last night she'd spend with him, Dakota was going to enjoy every second of it.

As he plundered her mouth, he ran his hands down her back to cup her ass. He lifted her off her feet so she wrapped around him. When he began to nibble down her neck she clawed at his shirt, trying to get it off.

Kieran carried her away from the table. Instead of taking her to the bedroom, he set her down in the middle of the desktop before clearing the surface of his work. Standing between her legs, he pushed her until her back was flat against the surface.

She kept her gaze on his as he lifted her shirt up and bent to run his tongue from her navel to her throat. Dakota gasped as she shivered. The warmth of the room kept her from being cold but goosebumps were breaking out all over her body.

Kieran grasped the back of her knees and yanked her to the edge of the desk. She was now at the perfect height for him to rub his erection against her cloth-covered pussy.

Growing desperate, she grasped at him. Kieran caught her wrists and forced them over her head, flat against the desk. "Keep them there," he demanded.

She nodded.

His blue eyes were glowing again and the faint hint of fangs excited her as he pushed her shirt over her head. Next he ripped off her bra and tossed it over his shoulder. He lowered his mouth until his lips went down to her right nipple and sucked.

"Ugh," she managed, gripping his hair.

He lifted his head before he seized her hands and placed them back on the desk. "I told you to keep these here," he said as he forced them back in place.

Dakota grinned at him. "What if I don't?"

"Then I won't do this," he said before he dropped to his knees and spread her legs. "Without your pants." He began to mouth at her clit and pussy, and she cried out in annoyance.

She wanted, no needed, to feel his mouth on her.

"I promise," she told him.

Kieran grabbed her foot then removed her shoes and socks. "Lift your hips," he ordered.

Dakota complied, and he unsnapped her slacks then pulled them and her panties off. Once she was naked he stood back over her. Kieran kissed her deeply. By the time he pulled away, she was seeing spots in her field of vision.

"Now be a good girl," he said before he licked between her folds.

She screamed as he pleasured her with an intense focus that she'd never felt before. Kieran nibbled, sucked and fingered her while Dakota did her best to keep her hands where they were. No way was she going to let him stop.

He had two fingers plunging in and out of her pussy while he played with her clit with his tongue. Dakota rocked her hips, driving the need higher. As she climaxed her toes curled and she dug her fingers into the desk.

Kieran calmed her down by petting her damp body as he rose over her. He cupped her face and turned it. "I'm not ashamed of you," he said. "I'd be with you in front of anyone."

It was only then that she realized the windows were wide open still and if anyone in the rooms across had theirs open too, they would be able to see into the suite. And there she was on her back right smack in the middle of the living area.

She jerked but Kieran already had his hands on her hips.

"I can carry you into the bedroom," he said as he trailed his fingers up her stomach. "Or I will close those curtains. Last choice…" Kieran cupped her breasts. "I fuck you right here."

She shivered. "Yes."

Kieran chuckled. "I guess the choice is mine." He kissed her messily, giving her time to get her arms around his neck and hold him tight.

As they parted, Dakota peered up into his gorgeous blue eyes and wondered how she was going to get through to him. She didn't want to give this, him, up.

"Here?" he asked as he grasped his cock and leaned forward.

"Yes," she agreed.

He thrust inside with one long, smooth stroke. Since she'd already gotten off, her body was still tingling and the stimulation quickly had her gasping and crying out.

Kieran's eyes were closed as he plunged inside her. He lifted her off the wood and drove himself into her faster and harder.

"I won't break," she panted out. "Kieran, look at me."

After he'd complied, she smiled up at him. "Take me," she said.

He growled, his eyes glowing and his fangs dropping out. She just gazed up at him and knew that this was the side that he hid away from everyone else.

"More," she encouraged. Dakota wanted to know what he would do next given free rein.

Kieran snarled as he sped up. The desk rocked under her but she couldn't care less. It could splinter and break and they'd have to finish on the carpet. Did it really matter as long they finished together?

"K," she cried out as she reached orgasm.

He closed his eyes as he faltered, grunted, then came.

Chapter Five

Kieran held up a long, soft hotel robe for her. Dakota dropped the towel onto the bathroom floor before she strolled over to him. His blue eyes were shining with happiness but not in the same glowing way they did when he was turned on.

"Thanks," she whispered as she cupped his face and drew him down for a kiss.

He licked at her lips before he closed his mouth over hers. She leaned into his strong body, loving the electricity that ran between them. There had to be somewhere that she could find some more answers about Walkers. Dakota pulled up and peered at him. Or she could just ask. "More wine?" she questioned. Maybe she could get him drunk first.

"Sure." He helped slide her arms into the robe before tying it. "You look like you have something on your mind."

In the heat of the moment, Kieran had confessed feelings that they needed to address. She'd been ready to walk out of the door and he'd stopped her. That had to mean something. "I think we should talk."

He nodded then turned and grabbed the other robe from the hook.

Since he'd been quiet once they'd finished making love and showering, Dakota decided to give him a couple minutes. With her body still tingling from what he'd done to her earlier, she wouldn't mind a moment or two to think.

As she walked into the living area, Dakota glanced toward the large window. Her face was heated and she knew she was blushing. Kieran's seductive words had been the most erotic thing she'd ever heard. Maybe someone had been able to see them. She'd never really considered being into being watched before but at that moment nothing could have made her stop. And if anyone had been observing, they had to have been jealous. She grinned then walked toward the table.

She picked up the wine bottle and poured the rest into their two glasses. The minute Kieran stepped into the room she could feel him. Her shifter senses were already on high alert with her jaguar close to the surface, and while Kieran was quiet, Dakota knew he'd joined her.

"This is the last of it," she said as she walked closer.

"Thanks." He accepted the glass. "I can order another bottle if you want."

"No." She smiled. "Let's have this before we go to bed."

The look of relief that showed on his face confused her.

"What?" she asked.

Kieran took a drink as he kept his gaze on her. Courage? Or was he just thirsty?

"Kieran?" she asked.

"Remy and Caspar call me K," he told her. "If you want, you can too."

Nicknames? Hmm, I don't mind that at all. "Okay."

"I thought you might be upset about earlier," he said quietly. "It's one thing to get caught up in the heat of the moment but afterward..." He shrugged as he trailed off.

That's what he's worried about? "I loved every minute of it," she confessed. "You know I can get away from you if I really want, right?"

He stiffened, and she sighed. "Come here." Dakota grasped his hand to tow him toward the couch. "Sit."

She dropped down on the table to face him. She set her wine down then took his glass to put beside hers. He raised an eyebrow at her. Ah, there was her cocky Walker. She preferred him like that. And if she didn't bring up shifters, he seemed pretty content with things. Dakota could let the issue go but she'd also meant what she'd said earlier. Her jaguar was a big part of her.

"You've never been with a shifter before, have you?" she asked.

His lips quirked. "You do know one of my partners is a wolf right?"

"In bed, sexually, and you know what I mean."

Kieran shrugged.

"I didn't think so," she said. "Another Walker?"

"Why are you asking?" His tone had gone cool. No more joking around.

"I'm guessing that you've only slept with humans."

"If you have a problem with the way I made love to—"

"Shut up!" she interrupted him. Dakota didn't raise her voice but she did make sure to sound firm. "I've never had a better lover than you. As you probably already guessed. But that has nothing to do with what I'm trying to say."

Kieran sat back against the couch and spread his legs. The slit in the robe opened, and it was all she could do not to straddle his waist. But this was important and they needed to talk.

"If you want to throw me against the wall and ravish me, do it," she told him. "Just expect me to return the favor sometime."

"Or on a desk?" he asked as he grinned at her.

"Anytime," she agreed. "You don't need to worry about me. I am strong enough to knock you on your ass if I want."

He snorted.

"Don't underestimate me," she warned. "My point is, you may have to be careful with humans but I'm not human."

Kieran dropped his gaze.

"I'm not asking you to tell me what happened with the shifters," she said, gripping his hands. "Maybe someday you will. But you are going to have to accept my jaguar."

"Didn't we already have this conversation?" he asked as he yanked his hands from hers.

"Yes, sort of," she said. "But then you distracted me."

"So what do you want me to say?" he snapped.

"Nothing." She shrugged this time. "However, every time you try to change the subject or conveniently forget I'm a shifter, I will remind you."

"Why?" he asked softly.

"I won't pretend you're not a Walker," she responded. "I might not have any past issues— Hell, there's so much I don't know, but I won't try to see you as human."

He sat for a minute before he nodded. "You can ask me, you know."

"Ask?" she repeated.

"About Walkers," he clarified. "You've never met another?"

"No." She shook her head. "Our division doesn't have any Walkers. I guess without having any in the city, the bosses don't think we should."

Kieran frowned. "You have Walkers here."

She jerked back. "We do?"

"And they've talked to or worked with someone from the Organization."

Now it was her turn to frown. "How do you know this?"

His gaze went to the desk. "Can I tell you later? I'm working on something so before I spill anyone's secrets, I need to find out more."

Dakota understood, she didn't like it, but she understood. "If you need any help, you'll let me know."

"Promise." He leaned forward and closed his fingers over her wrist, tugging a little. "Now why don't you come sit on my lap?"

"Mmm," she said as she crouched in front of him. With her free hand, she parted his robe the rest of the way, revealing his renewed erection.

Dakota stroked his cock several times before she leaned forward and kissed him. Kieran wrapped his arms around her waist and pulled her forward. She had to let go of his cock as she landed on his lap. With nothing on under her robe, she slid her pussy against his shaft. He began to nibble along her neck as she rocked back. Dakota gripped his shoulders, digging her nails in as she lifted to her knees.

She felt his hand against her clit and wet folds. She didn't need any more stimulation. She was more than ready and willing. Dakota pushed back, knocking into his hand.

Kieran nipped her chin but he did start to press his cock into her. Dakota lowered herself down slowly until his shaft filled her deep. He was so long and thick that she hadn't been able to wait any longer.

He grabbed the tie of the robe and pulled it off before he pushed the cloth off her shoulders.

With her knees braced on the sofa cushions, she rose up before she slammed back down. They both groaned together so she did it again and again.

"Yes," he hissed while cupping her breasts and kneading.

Dakota threw her head back and rode him fast and hard. Her breaths quickened as sweat trailed along her spine.

"More," he said in encouragement.

Thanks to her shifter genes, Dakota could move at incredible speeds. Never before had she used her gift during sex, but she didn't have to worry about hurting Kieran. Instead she could allow herself to let go of all control. Only with Kieran had she ever even considered it.

Her damp palms fell off his shoulders so she draped her arms behind his neck to hold on. Kieran gripped her wrist as he thrust up, matching her swiftness.

Dakota's vision narrowed as lights flashed behind her closed eyes. She screamed as she climaxed.

Kieran held her tight as he plunged up into her lax body. His growl would have made any shifter proud as he came.

"Holy shit," she murmured once she could speak again. Dakota turned her head and saw that once again they'd been in full view of the window. She giggled. "We've got to remember to shut the curtains eventually."

"Yeah," Kieran chuckled. "Why don't you do that?"

She grunted. "No way, you're going to have to carry me to bed as it is."

He patted her back. "I think I can handle that." He lifted

her hips and his cock slid out of her. Dakota couldn't help but groan at the loss.

Without warning Kieran stood, still holding her.

"I didn't mean now," she complained.

"We'll be more comfortable in the soft bed," he told her.

"True," she agreed. Since his shoulder was right there, Dakota placed her cheek against it.

When they reached the bedroom, Kieran laid her gently on the left side of the mattress before he circled around and pulled the blankets back.

"Come on," he urged, waving his hand.

She grinned and climbed to the other side. Kieran bent then kissed her forehead.

"Do you need anything?" he asked.

Dakota rolled over so she was facing the other side of the bed on her stomach then patted the blanket. "Just you."

As he stripped off his robe—and why hadn't she gotten it off him earlier?—Dakota watched him. When he stepped nearer she held up the comforters. He slid in next to her.

"This is nice," she said as she snuggled close. "I love all the pillows and blankets."

"Me too," he agreed.

"Who would have thought you're a creature of comfort?" she teased.

"I'm cooler than most people," he told her. "I crave being warm. Like when I drink blood. So I do what I can to be comfortable."

It was the first time that he'd brought up drinking blood.

"Why don't you bite me?" she found the courage to ask.

"It's not like the movies," he said.

She laughed. "Yeah, that I understand." Dakota lifted up so she was sprawled between his legs and over his stomach. She could rest her chin on his chest, loving the fact that Kieran wanted her close. "So why don't you tell me?"

"I need very little blood," he said. "When I feed it makes the person sick. Why would I want to do that to someone I'm with?"

She closed her eyes with a sigh. "Damn, it sounds so romantic when you see it on the big screen."

"Or read about it," he agreed. "Real life doesn't work that way."

"Of course it doesn't."

"Get some sleep," Kieran said.

"Okay," she agreed. Hopefully he'd still be there when she woke up. Dakota pressed a kiss to his cool flesh. If there were any way that she could give him some of her warmth, she would.

Dakota didn't know how she would live with what he had.

Being a jaguar shifter was awesome. She was faster than humans with better eyesight, hearing and ability to scent. With the extra training that she'd received from the Organization, she had the best of both human and shifter worlds.

Someday she hoped to share that with Kieran.

* * * *

It was too easy to get into the underground parking garage of the building that the local Organization was using as a front. The guard hadn't even looked up as Kieran had pressed his back against a wall only five or six yards away. The guy was a shifter but he obviously wasn't expecting someone to try to sneak into the building.

If this were his own office, Kieran would have had a little fun with the guard but he didn't want to end up in lock-up for the night. Or early morning.

It was fifteen after three in the morning and he only had a few hours before he wanted to be back in his hotel suite. He had plans on how to wake up Dakota.

Staying in the shadows, he strolled right beside the concrete wall toward the elevators.

Kieran could hear the electrical hum of the security cameras so it was easy to stay out of their range. He ducked between cars until he could speed through the only area that he couldn't get through without the cameras spotting him. He didn't have a choice but to chance it in front of the elevators.

Instead of waiting for the elevator, Kieran pushed through the emergency stairway and closed the door quietly behind him. He took a deep breath as he listened. Inside he couldn't pick up any surveillance equipment. That was good. Kieran had expected to have to race up the stairs too.

He took his time walking up, thankful that the city ordinance laws required all businesses to have stairs to exit from in case of a fire. Kieran had already received the blueprints for the building in an email that Lettie had sent him. Plus she'd given him access codes that she'd added to the security system so he could get into all areas.

It was good to have sneaky and smart friends.

Kieran paused in front of the door to the hall that would lead to the offices. His plan was to first get a look at Dean's office before he searched for some files on the Walkers in the area.

He placed his hand on the door and pulled it open. First he stuck his head in and peered around. The floor was dark and quiet. There were a few security lights on in the hall but the actual offices were dark.

With his shoulders back and head held high, he strolled into the hall. If he snuck around, he had a bigger chance of getting caught. By acting like he belonged there, he hoped no one he might come across would question him.

In his pocket he did have an ID card that he could pull out that would stop him from getting arrested but that would blow his cover. It would also lead to a call to Caspar and possibly him being locked up since he shouldn't be in another division's headquarters without permission.

The office was larger than his own agency's with cubicles in the middle and glass-plated offices on both sides of them. Halfway down on the right, he saw Dakota's name on a door. Oh, he was tempted to rifle around but he'd already decided earlier to leave her out of his antics. Still he did peer inside and just take a quick look. With his advanced sight he had no problem seeing without turning on the lights.

He wasn't surprised to see the neatness since he'd already determined she'd be professional and orderly at work. Dakota just came across that way to him. There were a couple of pictures on a bookcase and he stalked forward to get a better view.

One photo looked to be from several years ago and was of her and two other young women. Dakota's hair was darker without the red highlights but her smile still shone. All three wore shorts, tank tops and a marathon number. Kieran didn't know if Dakota still entered races, which made him wonder about her life outside the Organization.

In all honesty he didn't have anything other than his job. Even his friends were from his agency. He didn't have hobbies or other interests. So there was no one to work out with or run in marathons together as partners. While he tried not to think about how often he was alone, Dakota had made him want that connection for the first time.

The second picture was of her and Dean as they stood in front of the building he was standing in. They were smiling. The date on the bottom left corner was the day they'd become partners, he knew from Dean's file.

Finally the last photo was a group picture with Dakota on the side with all ages of people. It had to be of her family since he could see the resemblance between Dakota and several of the other people.

Her desk only held a computer, keyboard and mouse, along with a green plant on the corner. As much as he really wanted to search her desk he turned and walked out. Next door down he found Dean's office.

Kieran had an office in his division's building but he was never in it. In fact, from the last time he'd been there he was pretty sure there was nothing on the walls, desk or anywhere else. He didn't think he even had a bookcase. He wasn't sure what that said about him.

Dean's office was a little messier than his partner's and he had no personal photos around. Kieran went straight to Dean's desk and started to open drawers. Because of his connection with Caspar, and from who his family were, Kieran's best bet for finding an agent who knew about the Walkers in town was Dean.

But why wouldn't he tell Dakota? That was what bothered Kieran the most. It also made him wonder what Alex, his boss and the other Walkers might be up to.

Kieran was torn since he wanted to talk more to Alex, but trust was hard for him. He barely managed it with his partners and boss.

Since he didn't hear anyone around, Kieran clicked on the desk lamp. He could see in the dark but it did strain his eyes. In the first two drawers were the usual office supplies. Kieran was growing disappointed. If he had to search anywhere else for files, he wasn't certain where to go next.

The bottom drawer was locked, and Kieran grinned. If Dean wasn't hiding anything, why would he have to lock it?

There were no keys anywhere close so he could either try to lift Dean's keys the next time they met or break the lock. If Kieran had to return, he would be putting himself at risk again. He yanked hard on the drawer. Wood splintered and he had his access. Kieran reached in and pulled out the file folders from the bottom. He set them on the desk, growing excited and finally getting some answers. Kieran opened the first one and frowned. He'd been expecting information on the Walkers in town. Instead the first page was a list of names with dates next to them. He slid his phone from his pocket and tapped the camera app. He took a picture before he turned to the next page and clicked on the camera again. The second page held names also but with physical descriptions and summaries.

Halfway down he saw his own.

Kieran Smith

Male, Day Walker, Six-three, blue eyes
Held nine years, eleven months, twenty-two days
Rescued June 21, 2006 by Caspar Westbridge. Joined Organization upon rescue, evaluation and training. High-level agent.

Son of a bitch! Anger washed over him and Kieran couldn't hold it back. His fangs dropped and he snarled. He didn't care if Dean or anyone else knew he'd broken in.

No one had the right to keep tabs on him. He'd been told by Caspar that his file had been completely expunged and that no one other than the people involved and Caspar's supervisor would ever know what had been done to him.

Kieran stood with the files in his hand.

"I take it you found what you're looking for?"

He spun toward the door in a fighting stance, dropping the files. The man in the entry was almost as tall as he was and built. He had black hair and dark brown eyes and reeked like a shifter.

With a growl, Kieran leaped over the desk and landed crouched midway between the furniture and door. He stood to his full height while rolling his shoulder so his entire bulk was obvious. No one would ever take him again. He wasn't a victim but a survivor.

"You need to calm down." The stranger held up his hands.

"Fuck you," Kieran spat. He stalked forward, every instinct screaming at him to take out the threat.

"My name is Marcello Sparro."

Like Kieran gave a damn what the guy's name was. All he knew was the man was between him and the exit. The stranger posed a danger to Kieran's freedom and Kieran couldn't allow that.

He lunged the last few feet but when he expected to knock into the shifter he only met air. Kieran howled in frustration as he turned to attack once again.

"Take a deep breath," the shifter advised. "Calm down so we can talk."

Kieran didn't want to speak to anyone. He'd trusted once before after his truck had broken down on the side of the road in the middle of nowhere. Instead of the help he'd needed, Kieran had been knocked out and had woken in a cage.

With a yell he sprung and tackled the shifter to the ground. Kieran punched him and the guy's head snapped back. Blood flowed from the shifter's mouth as he pulled his arm back for another hit.

The breath was knocked from him as Kieran was kicked in the ribs. Kieran rolled away but leaped to his feet as the shifter also rose.

"I'm not going to hurt you," the shifter said.

But Kieran had heard that before, many times. Kieran dove at the man's legs, and they flew into the wall. His elbow hit the ground hard as he landed, and he bit his lip since his fangs were still extended. Kieran grunted when the shifter grabbed his already aching arm.

"I am not your enemy. I am Caspar's boss," Marcello said.

Caspar's name broke through the haze of fear and desperation. Kieran gasped and tried to level his breathing. "Let go of me," he demanded. But he didn't trust this shifter. When Marcello didn't release him, Kieran slammed his forehead against the shifter's.

Kieran's arm was released, and he was instantly on top of the enemy. He pounded his fists in the shifter's face until he was grabbed from behind.

"Stop!" Marcello shouted.

He howled as he was yanked away from Marcello and started to fight the hold on his shoulders and arms. An arm went around his neck, cutting off his air supply.

Desperate, he clawed at the arm as he snapped his fangs when a hand came into view. Kieran's vision was darkening and he knew if he didn't get free, this would be the end. He dropped his weight against his holder but while they stumbled Kieran wasn't freed.

Tears leaked from the corners of his eyes as the fight was

slowly draining from him. He blinked when Marcello's face was in front of him.

"It'll be okay," Marcello told him. "Just relax. No one's going to harm you."

Lies, the shifters had always told him lies. When he'd first been captured, they'd said that if he gave them his blood he could go. That they only wanted to study it. Kieran had been a scared eighteen-year-old kid who had had no family and hadn't known what to do. But even after he'd given in, they hadn't released him.

Ten years of experiments, beatings, sexual manipulation and torture had followed. He couldn't go through that again. He would rather die than ever be put back in a cage.

Caspar. Had his boss sent him here to die? Was that why Remy and Angel had taken their vacation so far away? He was all alone in a city he knew nothing about. Maybe the Walkers from the hotel had something to do with his capture. They could all be working together. Kieran might have stepped on too many toes in the last several years.

He tried once again to get free but despair washed over him and made his arms heavy. They dropped to his side, and he knew he was on the verge of passing out.

Marcello was still talking but he couldn't hear or understand the words.

Was Dakota aware of what was going on? Had she set him up? It seemed impossible, but what did he know?

Kieran had trusted Caspar, and look at where that had gotten him. He let his head drop back and closed his eyes.

Please, he prayed. *Kill me. Just end it.*

There was no way he'd last again in captivity. He could only hope he wouldn't wake back up.

Chapter Six

The insistent ringing dragged Dakota out of a deep sleep. She rolled over and stretched out her arm to nudge Kieran so she could get back to sleep. When her hand met only empty bed she sighed but sat up. "Really?"

There was no one there to answer her, though. Kieran wasn't in the bed, room or adjoining bathroom. At least the ringing stopped.

She concentrated her hearing on the other rooms but she knew that there was no one else in the suite with her.

Once again, the ringing sounded and she groaned. With Kieran gone that meant it was her cell phone. She dragged herself out of bed and glanced around for her clothes. Ah, yeah, living room. She picked up the robe that Kieran had worn last night and pulled it on before she strolled into the other room.

While the curtains were closed, the rest of the area was just as they'd left it. Dakota walked over to her pants, which were on the floor in front of the desk. She rifled through her pockets until she found her phone. The time on the device said it was just after five in the morning.

Dean's name was flashing across her screen.

"It's early," she said as a greeting.

"We need you at the office," Dean told her.

"Why? What's going on?" she asked as she circled around the desk. Kieran's notebook was still open and his laptop was in sleep mode. She trailed her finger over the keyboard mouse and it powered up.

"We had a little problem last night," Dean said. "Sparro said you needed to get here."

Dakota frowned as the computer opened on Kieran's email and she read the subject lines. Someone was sending Kieran reports on her, Dean and other agents from her division. All the emails had been opened except for the one with her name. Kieran hadn't looked at it yet.

Would he do it now?

While she was mildly irritated, Dakota couldn't really blame Kieran for looking into them. Dean had started the battle when he'd let Kieran know that Caspar had asked them to keep an eye on him. She'd even thought about looking into Kieran herself.

"Are you listening to me?" Dean demanded.

Dakota jumped up and pushed away from the desk. "Sorry," she said.

"Just get here ASAP," Dean said.

"I'm on my way," she replied. Dakota disconnected before she started to gather her up her clothes. She rushed to the bathroom then turned on the water in the sink. Since she wouldn't have time for a shower or to go home for more clothes, she'd have to make do. Luckily she kept a spare bag in her locker at the office so she'd be able to change at some point.

It was rare for her boss to call her or Dean in, so whatever had happened had to be big. The toothbrush from the day before was still there so she quickly took care of her morning routine before she dressed.

Once ready to go, Dakota walked back over to the notebook that Kieran had left open on the desk to leave him a note. She picked it up and saw that he'd been working on something strange. His writing was horrendous but she did manage to pick up 'Walkers', 'hotel', 'group', 'Organization contact'. If she had the time Dakota would try to figure out what Kieran was up to. Had he found more Walkers in town? She hadn't heard about any cases involving Walkers in her city but she'd have to check when she got to the office.

If Kieran was onto something, she wanted to know about it.

Dakota tore off a page and wrote Kieran a quick note.

Had to run to office – see you tonight

Maybe she could take him out to dinner or another club. As much as she loved being with him in private, Dakota wanted to take him around her city and show him what only a local knew about. There was so much more than the tourist traps.

A few drinks and a nice dinner should go a long way to buttering Kieran up and finding out what he was working on.

She placed the note on the edge of the desk then hurried toward the door.

* * * *

Kieran held his head in his hands as he sat on the cot in a holding cell. He'd woken up locked in the small prison room and knew he'd fucked up. Luckily he was still in the Organization building, or guessed that he was. He could smell a mixture of humans and shifters, heavy on the shifter. Plus the setup was exactly the same as the holding cells his division used.

He didn't know how long he'd been out but from his headache it had been a while. Kieran healed rather quickly, and even quicker if he drank, but having his air supply cut off screwed with the blood flow and killed off the good cells while leaving the bad.

It pissed him off since he'd just fed and now he'd have to find another source. As soon as the assholes released him. Caspar wouldn't let them hold him for long. It wouldn't surprise him if his boss showed up either.

All he had to do was bide his time. Kieran stood with a growl, even though the sound and movement made his head pound harder. He walked over to the iron bars and gripped them. With all his strength he tried to bend them. It would take too much energy to get through but if he could mess them up, he'd at least feel better.

Plus he really didn't want to think at the moment.

Sure, he realized that he'd overreacted with the boss that had caught him sneaking around Dean's office, but there were questions, too many damn questions, which made him uneasy.

Dean had a file with his name and information on it.

No, he wouldn't think about that until he was back in his hotel room alone. He'd find out what Dean and the Las Vegas branch were up to. Although he might need to move rooms again. He wouldn't trust Alex or the other Walkers either until he knew who'd told Dean about what had happened to him.

He just couldn't figure out why Dean hadn't told Dakota anything. And Kieran was certain she wasn't aware of his past. If she did know, Dakota wouldn't have pressed him. Not only that, but Kieran could read people, and Dakota had the people closest to her hiding things.

It seemed like every time he had a plan, there was a new twist. He really needed Remy to get to town, and together they would figure it out. Kieran might not like having to need someone but at least he trusted his partner.

Fuck, he wasn't going to think about any of this. He pushed away from the bars, disgusted with his thoughts and the fact that he hadn't even made a dent.

He took a deep breath before he strolled to the cot and sat down. He leaned against the wall and stared straight ahead. Kieran knew how to play the game. *Do not let your enemies see you weak.* That was the first rule that Caspar had taught him.

So he'd fall back on his training. The locals hadn't seen anything like him yet. Kieran knew how to protect himself and those around him.

Dakota. He couldn't pull her into this until he knew what he was up against.

It wouldn't be easy to get her to give him space. Already Dakota read him better than most people. He'd think of something, though. The urge to protect her was strong inside him and he knew that meant more than just a passing relationship while on vacation.

He might only be there for two weeks but they'd find a way to make it work between them. They had to.

Wow, it's crazy how things have changed so much in less than twelve hours.

Kieran banged his head back against the concrete. He had to stop thinking. Period. He closed his eyes and concentrated on his breathing. When he'd been captured before, he would stare at the wall of his cage for hours.

The shifters had kept him in a steel cage inside a cold room with no windows and only a bare light bulb hanging from the ceiling. He'd never seen another room like that one. Thankfully, since he'd probably lose his mind if he ever encountered anything like that again.

As his breathing evened out, Kieran sank into old memories. The air around him grew cold as it had always been during his imprisonment. He'd been so starved that he had begun to think that he'd never feel warmth again.

His fangs dropped down against his will as the past pulled at him. He hadn't been able to control his fangs then either. Well, when he'd had them. The shifters had loved to yank his fangs from his mouth, causing him the most horrible pain he'd ever felt. Each time his fangs had grown back the shifters had been delighted. If he hadn't done what they wanted when they asked, the first punishment had always been the loss of his fangs.

His teeth ached as he reminisced. Kieran ran his tongue over them and cut himself on the sharp edges. Blood dripped down his throat, and even though he didn't get the same feeling from his own blood as he did when he fed from another, it helped to remind him that he wasn't still in that hell.

"Are you okay?"

Kieran lifted his head then opened his eyes to peer at Dakota as she stood in front of the bars. He nodded once.

"I have the key," she told him. "Let's get you out of there."

Kieran stood before he walked slowly toward the door. "How'd you know I was here?"

"Dean called me. Sparro explained to him what was going on and Dean came up here. I guess you were still unconscious. After that he phoned me and asked me to be here when you woke. They weren't certain what state you'd wake in," Dakota said.

"So they sent you?" Kieran asked, disgusted. The two men had actually sent her to handle him in case he was still acting crazy. That was cowardice and despicable.

Dakota laughed. "I was seen entering your suite by the agent who was helping us keep an eye on you. When you left and I didn't, he called Dean. My partner's not stupid and he knew there was something going on between us, so after he found out Sparro had you here, Dean informed me."

"Okay," he said. "Let me out."

Dakota raised an eyebrow. "Is everything okay?"

"I'm locked in a fucking cell," he snapped. "No, everything is not okay."

"Right," she said as she unlocked the cell door and yanked it open. "Come on."

When she tried to place her hand on his arm, he backed away. Dakota let her hand drop while frowning.

"I've had enough people touching me tonight," he said.

The hurt that flashed over her face tugged at his heart but he had to get her to back off. For her own good.

"Sure," she said quietly.

"Am I free to go?" he asked.

"Actually, my boss wants to talk to you," she told him.

"Of course he does," Kieran quipped.

"Let's get this over with," she said. "Then we can talk."

Kieran had no plans to talk to her until he'd sorted everything out, but he nodded.

She spun on her heel, leading the way from his cell. Kieran glanced around and saw the cameras in the narrow hall as they walked toward the elevator. He hadn't been awake for his trip down there and he wanted to memorize every inch of the building.

There was no way to know if he would have to break in again. If so, he would be more careful.

Dakota slipped her card through a reader, which opened the elevator. Kieran needed to get himself one of those cards. He'd pocket one of the other employee's on his way out. He was good at pickpocketing—just one of the many skills he'd picked up along the way.

Remy had actually been the one that had shown him that talent. It had turned out his partner had a colorful past and Remy loved to show off.

Inside the elevator, Dakota pressed the button to the top floor. Which of course was where the boss's office would be located. Normally Kieran wouldn't take a risk to gather intel on one of the top guys but this gave him an opportunity that he wouldn't miss.

Dakota remained silent the entire ride up. Kieran stared forward even though he could feel her peeking at him every few seconds. God, he wanted to reach out and pull her close. But he had to be strong.

The faint ding of the elevator as they reached the correct floor had her jumping. Kieran held back a smile. As soon as the doors opened, she strode through in a way he could only describe as determined. Damn, he wished he could read her mind. He had no idea what she was thinking but the way she strutted made him think he might not be able to push her away like he was planning.

In the gray-walled hallway, there were a few doors that were closed and he wanted to peek inside but there was no glass windows like there were in Dakota and Dean's office space.

They reached the end of the hall, and Dakota rapped on the door.

"Come in."

Dakota turned the knob before she looked over her

shoulder at him and winked.

Kieran had no idea what that was for.

As the door swung open Dakota stepped to the side and he entered. The man behind the desk appeared rumpled and the scowl put a smile on Kieran's face before he'd taken three steps forward.

"Mr. Smith," Sparro said in a calm cool voice.

"Yep," Kieran returned as he ambled to the guest chair. He dropped down to sit.

"Now that we're alone let's talk about what happened," Sparro said, leaning forward.

If he was trying to intimidate Kieran, it wouldn't work. This shifter might be powerful—Kieran could feel the forceful energy radiating off him—but better men had tried to rein Kieran in. "Sure," he said with a shrug.

"You broke into a highly secured building," Sparro said. "I don't know whether to be angry or impressed."

"It obviously wasn't *that* well secured," Kieran replied.

"And that's why I'm leaning toward anger," Sparro told him.

Kieran wondered briefly if yawning would piss the shifter off more or if he'd finally get to the point. "Should I be worried?" he asked with a raised eyebrow.

"You should be respectful," Sparro responded then grinned. "But if you were, I'd know you were up to something."

"Aren't I always?" Kieran questioned.

"Yes," Sparro agreed.

Kieran didn't know why Sparro thought he knew him but he could play this out. "So what do you want?" he asked.

"It's time to discuss a few things," Sparro said. "Like why Caspar told you to vacation here."

Try as he might, Kieran couldn't hold in his reaction. He jerked only slightly but when Sparro nodded Kieran knew his response had been detected.

"Yes, I know everything. Were you aware that I'm Caspar's boss? The man he answers to?"

Well, fuck. Kieran hadn't. He vaguely remembered that Sparro had said something similar during their fight but he'd been so lost in memories and panic he hadn't connected the words. "So?" Kieran said even though he didn't sound as cocky even to himself.

"*So* that means you answer to me too," Sparro told him.

Kieran snorted. "Read my contract. I don't work under anyone except Caspar."

"Actually," Sparro said. "You should have read the fine print. In Caspar's absence I can step in and you'll follow my directions. I can also reassign your partners."

"No," Kieran shouted as he stood. "I won't work with anyone else."

"Not even Dakota?" Sparro asked as he also rose.

"No," he repeated and crossed his arms over his chest. Kieran wouldn't let anyone separate him from Remy and Angel. As much as he had feelings for Dakota, she wasn't who he could work with. Maybe it was because Dakota called to a part of him that Kieran had long ago attempted to bury. He couldn't think of her as he did his partners. In danger and always up against numerous opponents. Logically, he knew she did the same job he did but there was no way that he'd be able to deal with it on a day-to-day basis. He was too protective over her.

"And if I don't give you a choice?" Sparro asked.

"I'll quit," Kieran said. There was no question what action he'd take. He wouldn't let anyone push him around. Even if it meant losing Remy, Angel and Caspar, he would never let anyone have control over him again.

"That won't happen," Sparro said as he came around the desk.

Kieran growled as his fangs dropped. "I don't work for you."

"Yes, you do," Sparro replied.

A knock came from the door, and Kieran spun so he could see both Sparro and the entrance. He wasn't going to let Sparro trap him again.

"Perfect timing," Sparro said with a smile. "Come in."

Kieran backed up until he felt the wall behind him. There were two large windows behind Sparro's desk that he could jump from. He wasn't so far up that he'd break his neck if he made the plunge, but it would hurt. Still, that would be better than going back down to the cell.

If he ran, would that put Dakota in danger? It *was* her boss that Kieran needed to get away from, and Sparro could try to use his relationship with Dakota to trap him. He hoped Dakota would be okay. He could try to circle back around and search for her but that would be pushing his luck. She'd told him over and over that she could take care of herself. Well now might be the time that she'd have to prove it. Somehow the entire night — or morning, he wasn't even sure what time it was — had gotten fucked up.

Kieran sucked in a sharp breath when the door was opened and Remy strolled through. His partner's gaze went directly to him and he smiled.

"You okay?" Remy asked.

He nodded but remained silent. He knew Remy should have been hitting town today but since Sparro appeared to have expected Remy, Kieran didn't feel any better. Actually his anxiety grew. He slid along the wall, edging closer to the window.

"Don't!" Remy held up his hands. "I know what you're thinking, Kieran. Just let me explain."

"You have two minutes," Kieran told him. The feeling of betrayal burned inside him and Kieran was close to losing control. He needed to get to a phone and call Angel. If anyone could fix this clusterfuck that he'd made, it would be her. She understood him since she was also a Walker. Even though she had not had issues with shifters — hell, she had mated one — Angel always stood by him.

In all his worries, Kieran would never have thought that Remy would go against him and side with shifters. Kieran had put more stock in their partnership than Remy must have.

His eyes burned but Kieran hadn't cried since his rescue and refused to do so right then. Remy took a step forward. Kieran growled at him, keeping him back.

"I was just about to the city limits when I got a call from Caspar," Remy said. "He told me about your break-in and hoped I'd get here before you woke. I drove over a hundred miles an hour to get here so quick."

"Caspar called you?" Kieran asked Remy although he looked at Sparro.

"One of Caspar's employees breaks into my office, I'm going to give him a call," Sparro replied. "Shall we sit, gentlemen?"

Kieran glanced at Remy before he crossed his arms over his chest. Remy grinned then strolled over and copied Kieran's stance.

Sparro shook his head. "Caspar warned me about the two of you."

"And still you started this conversation with threatening me," Kieran said.

"I actually didn't," Sparro argued. "But I will admit our little talk did take an unexpected turn. I suspect that happens a lot with you."

Since Caspar always said the same thing, Kieran couldn't argue with Sparro.

"I'd like to talk about why you broke in here and what you found," Sparro told him.

"I was being followed by one of your agents." Kieran shrugged. "I was taught to know your enemy."

"But Dean's not your enemy," Sparro said. "He's your boss's nephew."

Remy stiffened next to him, but Kieran didn't take his attention from Sparro.

"Being Caspar's nephew does not mean he isn't my enemy," Kieran said. "That actually makes it even more suspicious."

"He was following you under Caspar's orders," Sparro told him.

Kieran lifted an eyebrow. "Not officially. So that equals suspicious."

"You're impossible," Sparro snapped as he stalked back to his desk. "It's not even seven in the morning and I want a drink."

Remy snorted.

"Something to say, Agent?" Sparro asked Remy.

"Nope," Remy replied with a grin.

"The reason Caspar asked Dean to keep an eye on you was because he didn't want anyone to know who or what you are before we'd decided on your future with the Organization." Sparro sat at his desk and waved his hand to the chairs in front of him. "I suggest you both sit so we can get on with this."

Kieran wanted to stay where he was to just be difficult, but Remy grabbed his arm and pulled him across the room. Once he was seated, Kieran leaned forward. "Fire me," he challenged. "See if I care."

"If I was to terminate your employment, I have no doubt that you'd stay in town just to make my life miserable."

"Well," Kieran drawled, "that's true." It also wouldn't be the only reason but Kieran wasn't sharing that.

"Instead I'm moving up my timetable," Sparro stated. "As soon as your vacation is up, you'll be transferred to this office. Under my authority."

"You can't do that," Remy shouted as he jumped up from his seat.

Kieran shot out his hand and yanked his partner back down.

"I can and I am," Sparro told him.

"He has partners, a boss and a job," Remy said. His voice had turned gritty by the end of his sentence as his wolf rose to the surface.

Kieran needed to get control of this conversation or Remy would get fired along with him.

"Does he?" Sparro questioned. "Is there anything you'd like to tell Kieran?"

"Don't try to turn this around," Remy demanded. "You're trying to take him from us and I won't let you!"

While Kieran had no idea what Remy needed to tell him and how Sparro would know, he couldn't let this go on. "Remy, let me take care of this."

Remy dropped back in his seat with a grunt. "Go ahead. You've been doing so well." He waved his hand.

Kieran laughed. He really hoped Remy hadn't betrayed him because damn, he liked his partner. If what he'd said was true and Caspar had called Remy, his partner's appearance here made sense.

It was hard but he had always trusted Remy and he needed to continue to do so.

"Oh, you misunderstood," Sparro said pleasantly. "Kieran won't be coming alone."

"You're transferring my team?" Kieran asked. That wasn't the worst news he'd ever heard. He could figure out what was going on with the Walkers in town while still seeing Dakota. There was only one problem. "I work for Caspar."

"Caspar has accepted a very important undercover assignment that will keep him busy for the next several months," Sparro informed him.

"Caspar doesn't work in the field," Kieran argued.

"This isn't something he could turn down," Sparro said. "He asked for this, as a matter of fact."

Alarm bells began to go off in his head. Caspar had once told him that he'd screwed up big and had been taken out of the field. Nothing would ever get him to work the streets again.

"No," Kieran said. "He can't."

Sparro sighed. "I tried to talk him out of it."

Kieran heard the sincerity in Sparro's voice. For just a moment Kieran felt something more than suspicion. Caspar had shared a lot with Kieran back when he'd been trying to earn Kieran's trust. But Kieran had never been able to get the full story of what had happened on Caspar's last mission. And Caspar hardly ever spoke about Sparro.

Actually, Kieran was really trying to remember anything Caspar might have said about this shifter in front of him.

"He's finishing a task that he started long ago," Sparro told him.

"I won't let him put himself in danger," Kieran said.

"Me either," Remy agreed.

"Well, as he's on his way here, I'll let you attempt to change his mind. Although I doubt you'll be successful."

"When will he be here?" Kieran demanded.

"Should be late tonight," Sparro said. "In the meantime let's talk about your new roles within the Organization."

"I won't agree to anything without talking to Caspar," Kieran said.

Sparro nodded. "Monday morning you will report here to me. I'm sure you can find your way inside."

Kieran grunted, not rising to the bait. He'd be doing a whole hell of a lot more than just showing up for work. Kieran still hadn't figured out what Dean was up to and why he had his file. Now he needed to know about Caspar's last assignment, deal with the Walkers at the hotel and somehow figure out what was going on with Dakota and him. Oh, and Remy was hiding something also. Just a few simple tasks.

He snorted as he stood. "Sure thing." He circled around the chair to stride to the door. When Remy didn't join him, he paused to look over his shoulder. "Remy?"

His partner's gaze was still on Sparro.

"Come on, Remy," he urged. "We need to talk."

His partner rose slowly to tower over Sparro. When he placed his hands on the top of Sparro's desk and leaned forward, Kieran prepared to launch himself at his partner.

"I don't know what you're trying to do but if you hurt anyone I care about, I'll bring my entire pack down on you," Remy threatened.

Sparro shook his head. "Calm yourself, wolf."

Kieran knew before Remy started to growl that Sparro had said the wrong thing.

The lion shifter got to his feet as he snarled. "You forget your place, pup. You are obligated to me by your blood. I own you, or your pack will suffer my wrath."

Remy lunged but Kieran was able to wrap his arms around his partner's middle and lift him off his feet. He ran out of the room, carrying Remy, before slamming the door behind him with every ounce of strength he had left.

"What the fuck are you thinking?" Kieran demanded as he slammed Remy against the wall.

"He's up to something!" Remy shouted.

"No shit!" Kieran replied. "Let me figure it out."

Remy took a deep breath before he banged his head against the wall. "Fine. Let go of me."

Kieran released him then took a step back. He eyed his partner. For the first time he noticed how tired his friend looked. "You need some sleep," he said.

"Yeah," Remy laughed. "You're not looking too good yourself, buddy. You need to drink."

He hadn't forgotten that he had to get blood. The headache that he hadn't quite managed to get rid of was a constant reminder. "I will."

"Don't be an idiot," Remy snapped. "Take my blood."

"No," he refused.

"Really?" Remy pushed off the wall as he glared at him. "You don't trust me?"

That wasn't one hundred percent true but he didn't want to get into anything right then. "You haven't checked into your hotel yet?"

"No," Remy said. "I came straight here."

"Do that," Kieran ordered. "Take a nap and meet me for a drink later."

"What are you going to do?" Remy asked.

Kieran glanced at Sparro's door. Kieran couldn't share his plan just yet. "I'm going to take a walk before I go back to my room and rest myself."

"Right," Remy said as he followed Kieran's gaze. "Text me later on where you want to meet up."

Kieran nodded.

As Remy strode past him, Kieran drew in a long breath. As tired as he was, he had a lot of work to do. He gave one last look to Sparro's closed door then he headed for the stairs. He'd take the long way down to see if he could gain more intel before he left the building.

He stalked down the hall and as he turned the corner he froze. And there she was.

Dakota leaned back against the exit grinning. "I knew you'd come out this way."

Kieran started walking again, admiring her. She'd changed clothes from when she'd gotten him out of the cell. Her hair was still damp so he could only guess that she'd showered somewhere in the building while he'd been in with Sparro.

"You think you know me?" he asked as he reached her. He breathed in her clean sweet scent and grew hard.

She licked her lips, and he followed the motion. If she was playing him, Dakota was damn good with her acting.

"I don't know what you're doing here or what my boss wanted with you but I don't think that's the only thing wrong. You've been weird since I released you."

How long had it been since he'd vowed to protect her by leaving her alone. "It doesn't matter. I'm leaving."

"What?" She placed her hands over his heart.

"I'm leaving," he repeated.

"You're going back to your hotel?" she questioned, but the way her voice wavered Kieran was sure she already knew his answer.

"No," he said softly.

"You can't leave me," Dakota said. "We're not done yet."

Kieran gripped her wrists. "We are now." He moved her out of the way before he pushed open the stairwell door and walked through it.

He heard her breath catch. As much as it tore at him, he didn't have a choice. Kieran would make it up to her but first he needed answers. If Dakota were with him, he'd be putting her at risk.

It was one thing to trust her with her own people. The Organization wouldn't kill her. He couldn't say the same about the Walkers or whatever Caspar had gotten himself into.

If Kieran ended up working with her, then he'd be able to really have something with her. They still had hurdles to overcome, her shifter status being the biggest, but if he was going to go all in, he'd have to accept every part of her.

She'd been right when she'd accused him of trying to forget that she was a shifter. Seeing her every day at work would be a constant reminder since she'd either have to use her senses around him or even shift into her jaguar.

He stomped down the stairs, not caring to be quiet like he normally would. He needed to find food then get back to his suite. The best option would be to check out but that would take him away from the Walkers. As long as Remy stayed off their radar, he might be better off where he could keep an eye on them. Changing hotels wasn't the right move, he was sure now.

As he jogged down the stairs, he heard the door above him slam open.

"Kieran!" Dakota shouted.

He sped up and was down the last couple of floors before she'd cleared the landing. Kieran ended up in the parking garage. He leaped over a car then hopped the concrete barrier. His power was waning but he could lose her.

The morning was too bright and he wished he'd brought his sunglasses. He needed to feed.

Kieran stopped a block away to gather himself. Being in a crowded area would work to his advantage. He would hunt.

Chapter Seven

Dakota leaned closer to her monitor as she clicked out of one file and opened another. She was still steaming from her encounter with Kieran earlier so when she pressed her mouse a little harder than normal, her nail broke.

"Son of a bitch," she cursed under her breath.

If she'd only caught up to him, Dakota would have given Kieran a piece of her mind before letting him know she knew what he was trying to do. He was pushing her away and Dakota was not going to allow it.

She understood that he'd had a rough morning but that was no reason to push her away. Dakota wasn't weak, and he was going to finally have to accept that. If he thought he needed to protect her, he was going to have to learn how it was going to be between them. She was just as strong as he was and wouldn't back down from a fight.

When she'd first met Kieran, she'd known he was stubborn but she had been certain the connection they'd shared had changed things. *Oh how wrong I am.*

Not finding the report she wanted in the file she'd chosen, she moved onto the next one. If Kieran was going to act like a jackass, she'd give him time to cool down before she went searching for him.

In the meantime she wasn't needed in the field, so she was going to do a little digging around to find out more about Walkers. The more intel she had, she was hoping the better understanding she'd get about how to handle her man.

"Ah," she murmured. Here was a case from back in the seventies. As she read through she grew more and more frustrated. It was obvious that key details had been deleted from the dossier. How was she going to learn anything if the secrets around the Walkers remained?

"Hey."

Dakota jerked her head up as she heard her partner's voice. "Oh, hi," she said as she leaned back in her chair. "Finally done with your secret meetings?"

Their boss had called Dean into his office as soon as Kieran and the wolf shifter had left. Dakota hadn't even known that Kieran's partner, Remy, was in town but Dean seemed pretty knowledgeable about everything going on. She felt very left out.

"Mind if I shut the door?" he asked.

Dakota lifted her eyebrow. "If I say no, are you going to take me to one of the cells?"

"That's not fair," Dean argued. "I had nothing to do with Kieran getting locked up. He attacked our boss." He went ahead and closed her door before he strolled to one of her guest chairs.

"What was he doing in your office in the first place?" she questioned.

"I don't know for sure," Dean replied.

"But you have an idea," she guessed.

"It doesn't matter," Dean said. "That's not what I came to talk to you about."

Dakota scoffed. "What's going on with you? You've been acting weird before Kieran even got here."

"I know," he agreed. "And I'm sorry that I didn't talk to you before now."

The seriousness in his voice was not what she'd expected. Dean was usually lighthearted and loved to joke around. "What is it?"

He took a deep breath before he spoke. "About six months ago, I called my uncle to talk about my future with the Organization."

"Why?" she asked. "We don't have a choice in our service."

"But that doesn't mean I can't change where I serve,"

Dean said.

"You want out of the field," she said for him. She'd always known that Dean's heart hadn't been in the same place as hers but he was good at his job.

"I never wanted in it," he confessed.

Damn it, Dakota didn't want to lose her partner but Dean was also her friend. "What can I do to help?"

He smiled. "You're already doing it."

"What do you mean?" she questioned. She hadn't even known he was trying to get reassigned.

"The reason Caspar sent Kieran here and wanted me to watch out for him is because Caspar will be taking a short-term job in the field. He needs to find a place for Kieran that he'll fit in. Kieran won't work for anyone other than Caspar and hopefully Sparro. I guess it hasn't been easy to place him."

Dakota snorted. "He does seem to enjoy pissing people off."

"Yeah." Dean nodded. "If he'd attacked anyone other than Sparro, they'd be dead. But since Sparro has dealt with some of the most dangerous agents, Caspar sent Kieran here."

"They want to transfer Kieran?" she asked.

"Yes, and his partner. Not only can Sparro handle them but with the Walkers in the city organizing, we need more of their kind."

"Organizing?" Dakota jumped to her feet. "What do you know about that?"

"Sparro was contacted by a Walker that lives here and has several others in his employment. They've stayed in the shadows for the past several years but they've been more active lately," Dean said.

"So we need Walkers on our team. And Kieran will be the first," Dakota said. "Does he know?"

Dean nodded. "Sparro told him today."

And right after that, he'd told Dakota he was leaving. "Did he accept?"

"He wasn't given a choice. Monday morning they report for duty here."

She wasn't so sure that Kieran was on the same page as her boss and Dean. She grabbed her bag from beside her desk. "I have to go."

"Wait!" Dean rose and placed his hand on her arm.

"What? I need to talk to Kieran."

"We need to talk about you and him," Dean told her. "Sit back down."

"Why?" She pulled her arm from his.

"I know you have feelings for him," he said. "I'm worried about you."

"There's nothing to be worried about," she assured him.

"You're falling for a guy that you know nothing about," Dean said. "He's dangerous, Dakota."

"I know what I'm doing," she said. "Kieran is a good man."

"Who suffers from PTSD from years of torture," Dean argued.

"How do you know about that?" she asked. Since her chair was there, she went ahead and dropped into it.

"I was given his folder so that I could give my opinion on whether or not he'd be helpful with the other Walkers," Dean explained.

"And how would you know that?" she asked.

"Because for the past month, I've been their contact within the Organization."

She stiffened. "Just how many secrets are you keeping, Dean?" she accused.

"It's not like that," Dean said as he held up his hands. "I had to find a replacement and the only way I could was to dig into the only agent who isn't here by a blood bond. I was doing what I was ordered."

"So that's just supposed to make everything better?" she asked.

"I'm just trying to tell you why I've done the things I have," Dean said.

"All I've gotten from this conversation is that you didn't trust me and worked behind my back to get what you wanted. Well, congratulations." Dakota stood. "Now, if you don't mind, I have a few errands to run."

She picked her bag back up before she stormed out of her office. This was such bullshit! After all the years that she and Dean had been partners and friends, he was just pushing her aside to get what he wanted.

Dean had to know that she would have supported him every step of the way. Or maybe he hadn't since confiding in her wasn't a step he'd taken.

Her partner had also found out things about Kieran that she wanted to know. She wouldn't ask him, though. If she had to wait for the rest of her life, one day Kieran would tell her what had happened himself.

Instead of taking the elevator like she normally did, Dakota pushed the stairway door hard, letting it slam against the wall. She thundered down the stairs as her mind whirled.

Dean was leaving her. Kieran might or might not be staying. No matter how she looked at what the morning had brought, changes were happening and she had no control of any of it.

Her jaguar was closer to the surface than it'd been in months. She needed to get out into the wild so she could let her animal loose and hopefully gain some clarity. There was nothing like shifting then running.

Just letting the world around her revolve for the time being. Until she came up with a plan, Dakota was at a loss for what to do.

She wished she was back in Kieran's comfortable bed with his arms tight around her. She had gone to sleep in heaven and woken up in hell. Dakota really needed someone to talk to. Too bad the only person who she really wanted to see had already taken off on her.

After her run she was going to hunt him down. If she wasn't in a better mood, he might just regret her having to find him.

* * * *

Kieran strolled through his hotel entrance, feeling once again revived and ready to battle. He wasn't going to let Caspar go off on his own without knowing exactly what he was up to.

His boss had been out of the field for far too long. There was no way Lettie would have access to a case that Caspar was involved in so he needed his boss to tell him what was going on himself.

Also he had to decide what to do about the Las Vegas boss, Sparro. Kieran had the beginnings of respect for the man. He'd fought well when Kieran had attacked him but that didn't mean he wanted to transfer.

Then there was Remy. His partner had been hiding something as well, but now that Kieran had had time to cool down, he felt guilty for doubting his friend. Remy had proven that Kieran could trust him, and no matter what Remy had to say Kieran would support his buddy.

Last, there were the Walkers in the city who he was still suspicious of. They had contacted him for a reason, and Kieran had never met a Walker not involved with the Organization that didn't hurt people.

He searched for Alex in the throng of tourists and guests. If his bad luck was holding, he should run into the Walker at any time. Prepared or not.

"Mr. Smith."

Right on schedule. He stopped before he turned and faced the Walker. "Good morning," he greeted.

"I see you're just arriving but if now is a convenient time, my boss would like to speak to you," Alex said.

Kieran wondered how the conversation would go if he refused. If he had more time to spare, maybe he'd try it but he really wanted to get to the bottom of what Alex and his boss were up to.

"Sure," Kieran agreed.

"Follow me, please." Alex waved his hand before he led

the way through the casino floor.

Around the main floor, away from the tables, was a narrow dark hallway that Kieran had noticed but hadn't had the opportunity to explore yet. As Alex strode ahead of him, Kieran saw more security personnel in the area. So this had to be where the big boss kept his office.

As the noise of slots and people shouting filtered away, Kieran was grateful. He really didn't like being surrounded by so many possible threats. The door they passed was closed and he didn't pick up any sounds coming from inside.

"This is where he keeps some of the staff's offices as well as a few meeting rooms," Alex said as they walked.

At the end of the hall was an elevator. Kieran glanced around in confusion. Alex pulled out a key card from his pocket. "This is a private elevator that will lead us to the boss's floor. You can't access his area any other way."

"Warning?" Kieran asked.

"Your reputation precedes you," Alex said with a smile.

"Then why show me this?" he questioned.

"My boss doesn't think that you'll trust us until you know everything. I've been ordered to answer all your questions honestly and to the best of my ability," Alex said.

"That answer just makes me more suspicious," Kieran told him.

Alex laughed. "That's what I said. But Jackson said once the two of you met that you'd understand."

The elevator arrived, and Kieran stepped inside in front of Alex. The interior was sleek even in the small space. There was only one button on the wall next to another card swipe. Alex slid the same card through then pressed the button. There were no floor numbers to tell Kieran where they were headed. He picked up the faint mechanical hum of a security camera. Kieran raised his head and stared right into a camera. He would show strength.

"I'm beginning to think that my boss was right about you," Alex said.

Kieran didn't respond. No matter what they'd learned about him, they didn't have a clue about who Kieran really was.

The elevator came to a soft, silent halt before the doors whooshed open. Alex held his hand out. "After you."

Kieran stepped onto a thick and soft gray carpet, his feet sinking in. He smiled. It appeared he wasn't the only one who liked extravagant comforts. He stepped inside a modern-looking waiting room. There were black leather couches, stainless steel fixtures and windows everywhere. The openness of the entry was what he would have designed himself. A young woman with her blonde hair tied up in a knot smiled at him.

"Hello, Katy," Alex greeted.

"Good morning, gentlemen. The boss is ready for you."

"Thanks." Alex slapped Kieran on the back. "Let's not keep him waiting."

This time Kieran allowed Alex to go first. Behind the young woman two doors were closed. She rose then pulled one open. Kieran nodded to her as he passed. She was human, at least, and that made him feel a little more comfortable. "Thank you," he murmured to her.

She beamed back.

Once he stepped inside the office, he smiled then turned in a circle. Kieran was still buzzing a little from the blood he'd taken, and walking into the comfortable room was heaven.

A tall, muscular, good-looking man rose from his desk and started toward him. Kieran froze in shock before he had a memory flash from years before.

He'd been alone for so long that Kieran didn't even mind when the guards taunted him because at least he got to look at another person. He heard the outer door open and stiffened. It was time for his one meal a day so that meant the guards were coming to get him for another test.

It was so hard to keep his body from shaking. Kieran didn't want to show them fear but he was terrified all the time.

Never knowing what they were going to do to him left Kieran in a constant state of anxiety. On the good days, they'd merely take blood and allow him to return to his cage. Then there were the bad days when they'd experiment on him. Sometimes they'd cut him or use crazy instruments, but the worst was when they'd try drugs on him.

Kieran was only eighteen and he'd never tried anything more than a beer. No hard alcohol or street drugs. Now he'd possibly been injected with every imaginable concoction. Some made him violently ill, aroused or crazy. Kieran just wanted to close his eyes and fade away to never wake up again.

Too bad something inside him refused to just give up. God, he was so damn tired.

The guard's footsteps echoed around the concrete walls as they walked closer. There was also a dragging noise that he couldn't place. Fuck, what could they be planning for him now?

When two guards came into view, Kieran didn't understand. They had someone else with them. The stranger was being held up by the two shifter guards and appeared to be unconscious.

The ugly, dark-haired piece of shit wolf shifter who liked to tease Kieran with food snarled at him as he passed Kieran's cage. In his mind Kieran had come to calling the guards not by name but by their shifter animal – wolf, lion, bear, panther and falcon. To his right was another cell just like Kieran's – four feet tall and six feet deep, made out of stainless steel bars going all the way around. The guards pulled open the door before they dropped the new guy onto the floor. The stranger's head smacked the floor hard, and the sound made Kieran's stomach lurch.

After they'd chained and locked the now occupied cage, they returned to stand in front of Kieran's cell.

"Think they're finally done with this pussy?" Wolf said to his partner.

"I don't see why they'd keep him," Bear replied.

Kieran didn't show a response to their words. They'd beaten all smartass comments out of him after the first few months.

Fuck! Kieran didn't even know how long he'd been imprisoned. Years and years had to have passed. At first Kieran had tried to *keep track of the days but when he'd gotten into the hundreds, he'd grown so depressed he'd stopped.*

"He's broken," Wolf said with a sneer. "I hope they let me take him out."

As they walked away, Kieran kept his gaze on the new prisoner. When he couldn't hear them anymore, Kieran dragged himself from the back wall of bars to where his cage butted up against the stranger's.

The first thing he noticed was that this new guy didn't smell like a shifter. It was such a relief that he collapsed against the bars.

"Hey!" he whispered, his voice was horse and his throat hurt. He never spoke to his captors but the shifters loved to hear him scream. "Hey, you okay?"

The guy moaned, turning his head toward Kieran. Dull blue eyes opened, and Kieran knew they were both in so much trouble. This man was a Walker like Kieran.

"It's okay, just breathe," the man from his past said.

Kieran blinked into awareness and realized he was on the floor with the same man he'd once shared years of hell with. Kieran had been locked up for over ten years and this guy had been with him close to three.

Three weeks before Kieran had been rescued, they'd taken this man away and he'd never seen him again. He'd been sure that his only friend during that time was dead.

"Jack?" Kieran whispered in confusion and shock.

"Hey, K," Jack said. He was on the ground with Kieran holding Kieran's head in his hands. "You okay now?"

"What are you doing here?" Kieran asked. He couldn't get his mind around what was happening.

"I'm here to talk to you," Jack told him. "Come on." Jack helped him to his feet before he lead Kieran to a couch.

Kieran looked around and noticed they were alone.

"I asked Alex to give us a minute," Jack told him.

"How long was I gone?" Kieran asked. Jack would know what he was talking about. Back in their cage days, they'd watched over each other after one of them was taken into the experimenting room.

"Only a couple minutes, but I knew you wouldn't want anyone else to see you like that," Jack told him.

"Thanks," Kieran said sincerely. He felt like the teenager he'd been when he'd first met Jack. After Jack had joined him, Kieran had regained some of his fight. He'd looked up to Jack for so long.

"Can I get you some water?" Jack asked.

Kieran nodded. He needed a few minutes to regain his composure. To remember that he was free and in control of his own fate.

While Jack strolled across the room to a mini-fridge behind his desk, Kieran took in the sight of his old friend. Jack had filled out into a pretty big guy. Kieran didn't know if he just remembered him so skinny or if Jack had done something to get so much stronger.

"Here you go." Jack handed Kieran a cold bottle of water.

"Thanks."

Jack sat next to him. "I didn't think you'd react that way. I was actually worried that you wouldn't remember me."

"What?" Kieran scoffed. "You saved me, why wouldn't I remember you?"

"When I was found in the bank of a river, naked and almost dead, I didn't have any memories. It wasn't until after several years of therapy that I knew for sure that I wasn't just having nightmares. I'd been held captive and tortured," Jack explained.

"I thought you were dead," Kieran confessed.

Jack gripped his shoulder. "Once I knew I wasn't just crazy, I went back to where a fisherman had found me and searched for months for where they'd kept us. I never found it."

"It wasn't long after you were gone that I was rescued," Kieran told him.

"By the Organization," Jack said.

"Yes," Kieran admitted.

"When I couldn't locate you, I went to every federal and local agency I could get into," Jack told him. "Then one night a man came to my house and told me that you were alive and doing well. I wanted to talk to you but he was worried it would hurt what you did now."

"Who was it?" Kieran asked even though he had a pretty good idea already.

"Your boss," Jack confirmed. "He said that you'd put it all behind you."

"I have," Kieran said. At least he'd thought so, but now, sitting beside his old friend, Kieran was colder than he'd been in years. It felt like back when he'd had no blood and had been starving.

"I almost stayed away when Alex told me that you were staying here. But then I figured that fate brought you to me." Jack smiled at him. "It's good to see you."

The hug was unexpected but Kieran returned it.

"Now," Jack said as he released Kieran. "We have a lot to catch up on."

Kieran nodded. "Like how you came to own a hotel like this and run a community of Walkers."

Jack laughed. "I guess I never told you that my family had money."

Well, it hadn't come up. They'd talked a lot during those long days and nights but since neither of them had expected to make it out, money hadn't been spoken about. "No, you left that out."

"I came here on vacation with my brother and loved the lights and how busy the city was. When I'm in town, I never feel alone," Jack said.

Kieran felt the same way but reacted differently to it. He actually preferred to be alone.

"I own several hotels over the world but this is my main base," Jack said.

"Wait." Kieran remembered something. "Alex called you Jackson."

"Yes." he nodded. "Jackson is my full name. After I recovered I never wanted to be the man I was during my time in captivity."

"I'll try to remember," Kieran said.

"Is it still okay for me to call you K?" Jackson asked.

"Yeah." Kieran shrugged. He didn't really care but since his closest friends called him that, Jackson deserved to as well.

"And you're still working for the Organization?" Jackson questioned. He leaned back, getting comfortable, which helped Kieran relax. Kieran wasn't used to so many emotional ups and downs. He was exhausted.

"I do," Kieran confirmed.

"You enjoy what you do?" Jackson asked. Something in his tone made Kieran think that Jackson wasn't just making small talk.

"I'm good at it. I like my partners," Kieran told him.

"Since I found out where you were, I've kept tabs on the Organization and can honestly say that you all do good work," Jackson said.

It made Kieran feel good to hear that. Jackson was someone he respected, much like he did Caspar. "Thanks."

"But I want you to know that you'll always have a place with me," Jackson said. "You could work in any of my businesses and be around others just like us."

"One of my partners is a Walker," Kieran confessed. "She's the only one I'm really connected to."

"You're also surrounded by shifters," Jackson pointed out. "I'd let you pick your own team to lead. I always need security, and with your experience you'd do great."

Kieran thought about Remy and Dakota. True, he hated most shifters but every now and then he found one that he was lucky to have met. Who was he kidding? He was grateful they even put up with him. He knew how much of a pain in the ass he could be.

Now that the Organization was talking to him about transferring—or ordering him to really—Kieran could still be with Dakota and wouldn't have to lose his partners. He'd have the same opportunity with Jackson.

"Of course you'd make more money as private security

than with what the Organization can pay," Jackson told him.

Money wasn't an issue for him. Kieran didn't spend what he made now. "That's a generous offer."

"But?" Jackson drawled out.

"I have a few things to think about. This is all happening really fast, and like I said I'm good at what I do," Kieran responded.

"It's an open-ended offer," Jackson said. "You can take me up on it anytime."

Kieran was relieved that he didn't have to answer right away. He hadn't even processed seeing Jackson again yet.

"You're overwhelmed," Jackson said. "And I can understand that. But even if you don't work for me, I'd like to stay in touch."

"Of course," Kieran agreed quickly. Caspar might think that he'd been protecting Kieran but his boss had some questions to answer. Well, more than what Kieran had already planned on asking him.

"You're still staying in the hotel?" Jackson questioned.

"Yes." Kieran wouldn't be checking out now. It would make it harder to put distance between him and Dakota but he'd figure something out. With the way he'd reacted to seeing Jackson again, he was embarrassed. It had just been a shock. He was glad Dakota hadn't been there to see him pass out. This was why he had to push her away. His life was just too damn complicated.

"You're still looking a little pale," Jackson said as he rose. "Why don't you go up to your suite and we can get together a little later. I'd still like to know everything you've done since you left that horrible place."

"That's a good idea," Kieran agreed as he pushed up from the couch.

"It's really good to see you." Jackson reached out and pulled him into another hug.

Kieran slapped his friend's back. "You too." He stepped back and grinned. "You don't look very much like you used to."

Jackson laughed. "I worked damn hard at that."

Kieran turned toward the door. "I'm going to take your advice and go up to my room."

"Wait! Let me get you my numbers." Jackson rushed back to his desk and lifted a business card. He scrawled on it before he walked back over to Kieran and handed it to him. "I wrote my personal number on the back. Call me and we'll have dinner tonight."

Kieran slipped the card in his pocket. "Will do." It was hard to turn his back on Jackson, a small part of Kieran wondering if this was all a dream and if he'd see his old friend again.

He reached out for the door knob and paused. Kieran glanced over his shoulder to just get one more look.

"It's really me," Jackson said with a smile.

Kieran nodded and he turned the handle.

"Hey, K," Jackson called.

"Yeah?" He glanced back.

"They never found the people responsible for what was done to us," Jackson said. "Do you ever think about that?"

"No," he replied honestly. "I wouldn't be able to sleep at night."

"We need to talk about it," Jackson told him. "I don't want to surprise you with it later so I just thought I'd warn you. If you don't want to know what I've found out, I won't tell you, but I think you need to."

"Okay," Kieran agreed. "We'll discuss it later."

He made his escape while he could. Kieran needed the peace and quiet of his own space. Even if that was in a hotel suite that didn't really belong to him.

Alex stood up from one of the reception chairs when Kieran stepped back out of the office. "I can take you back to your room from here so you'll know how to get back and forth in the future," he offered.

"I'd appreciate it," Kieran said. It was hard to look at Alex since Kieran didn't know what he had witnessed during his flashback, but he refused to show any weakness.

"This way." Alex waved him toward the elevator.

Kieran followed him, grateful when Alex didn't try to make conversation. The ride up to his floor was quick and silent. When the elevator doors opened, Alex held the door open for him.

"I hope to see you again," Alex told him.

"I'm sure you will," Kieran replied. He shuffled forward, his legs feeling like they weighed a ton. At his door, he fumbled with his key card but finally saw the green light allowing his entrance.

He sighed as he pushed inside before he locked the door behind him. Luckily the housekeeping crew had already been in and the suite smelled fresh and clean.

Kieran ambled straight for the bedroom. Once he passed the threshold of his room, he began to undress, dropping his clothes on the floor. He pulled the blankets down and crawled inside before yanking them back over his head. He was safe in his little nest. Kieran closed his eyes as fatigue began to take over him.

Chapter Eight

Dakota nervously fingered the key card as she stood in front of Kieran's suite.

She'd enjoyed her run in her jaguar form and was now a lot calmer so she hoped Kieran would listen to her before he tried to send her away. Dakota understood that Kieran was dealing with his boss going back into the field and a transfer but she was not going to allow him to push her away because things were changing for him.

If he'd just let her in with what he was dealing with she could help.

Now as she held the plastic card up to the reader she really hoped her lover was inside. "Come on. Be here," she murmured as she slid the key to his suite through the reader. She'd had to use her credentials to get a copy but she wasn't worried about breaking protocol.

The suite was quiet and dark. All of the lights were off and the curtains closed. After she'd taken a long run, she'd showered, dressed, packed a bag then headed here and it was already past noon. Unless he was somewhere else in the hotel, he should be here. He hadn't slept the night before and he had to be exhausted.

She closed the door silently behind her before she slipped the key card back into her pocket. The living area had been cleaned and smelled of lemon cleanser and wood polish. Just to make sure she was alone, Dakota strolled to the bedroom. As she got closer, she could hear a soft sound coming from inside. The noise was so faint it was hard to pick up even with her enhanced hearing.

Dakota peered around the corner of the threshold. In the

center of the bed, under the covers, Kieran was sleeping. His head and one shoulder were bare but the rest of him was buried below a large pile of blankets. The picture of the big, bad Walker nesting was enough to have a smile blossom.

Kieran was such an interesting man. At first he was rude and sarcastic but he really just was afraid to let anyone close. His attempt to push her away earlier was a clear indicator of this. She leaned against the wall and watched him. She didn't think she'd ever get tired of seeing Kieran like that. She wanted to climb up beside him and cuddle close but Dakota knew he needed his sleep and that she couldn't wake him. That didn't mean she was going anywhere until Kieran and she spoke, and he accepted that she was not leaving him.

Every part of her wanted Kieran, from her human heart to her Jaguar instincts. Sure, they had a lot to work out together, but she was a fighter and Kieran was hers.

Admitting the claim on him made her feel powerful.

Kieran turned onto his stomach while he made a low whimper. She narrowed her eyes as her protective instincts rose up. The man she'd decided to claim was not happy. She might not be able to scent him but it was obvious by the way he kicked his legs and grunted that the dream he was having was not a good one.

"Shh," she whispered as she walked to the far edge of the bed and sat. Dakota laid her hand against the back of his neck, finding Kieran cooler than usual. As a matter of fact, she now remembered that at the agency he'd been very pale. She was pretty sure that Walkers didn't get sick—or maybe they did, she still didn't know much—but it was unlikely due to the supernatural healing that rumors claimed they had. Still, something was off with him.

He grunted again, kicking his feet out, so she toed off her shoes before cuddling up to his side and murmuring softly. Once her body brushed his, Kieran calmed and settled. Dakota wrapped her arm around his waist before she laid her head on the back of his shoulder. Kieran's breathing changed and she knew he'd woken up.

Kieran turned his head so his face wasn't buried into the pillow but he didn't otherwise move. "I thought I told you I was leaving," he said, his voice rough from sleep.

She snorted. "And I thought you knew me better than that," Dakota responded.

He sighed and she already knew that she'd won. Oh, Kieran might make another attempt at getting rid of her but he didn't really want her to go anywhere. If she had any doubt, she wouldn't be chasing him, no matter how much her shifter instincts would have tried to make her. But Kieran wanted her just as much as she did him.

"I'm not going anywhere," she promised. If she repeated the words over and over, someday she hoped he'd realize she was telling him the truth.

Kieran began to roll over, which made her have to sit up slightly. She waited until he was on his back before she covered one of his legs with hers and put her chin on his chest. The look she gave him was pure challenge. She was not leaving the bed, suite or him.

He shook his head. "There is some stuff going on around me that I don't want you involved with," he told her.

Dakota lifted an eyebrow. "Illegal?"

"No," he answered. "I wasn't sure at first but now I'm pretty certain no laws are being broken."

"Then let me help," she pleaded. "We might not have known each other for long but the connection between us is strong. I know you feel it."

"Of course I do," he said.

When Kieran looked away, Dakota gripped his chin so he had to meet her gaze. "You have to stop running eventually. You can trust me."

"I want to," he whispered then shook his head again. "This was supposed to be a stupid vacation to waste time until my partners were ready to get back to work. Now everything in my life has changed."

"That doesn't have to be a bad thing," she said. Dakota waited a few moments to see how he would reply. When he just continued to peer at her, she decided to push in a direction that shouldn't cause him stress. "You haven't told me about your partner before. I saw him in the office earlier."

"Remy," Kieran said. "He was headed here to do me a favor but after your boss had me locked up, he came to check on me."

Dakota decided to ignore the 'your boss' comment for now. He was opening up to her and she didn't want to jeopardize anything by reminding him of one of those big changes. "He's a shifter."

"Yeah," Kieran said "Wolf. But we've been working together for so long that I don't even think about it anymore. He's my best friend."

"So your best friend and the woman you're sleeping with are both shifters," Dakota said. "For someone who seems to hate shifters so much that's very interesting."

"Or a cosmic joke on me," Kieran said.

She laughed. "Perhaps."

"I didn't want to be partnered with him. I fought it for several months. I was already teamed up with Angel and we were doing just fine."

"Angel?" She hadn't heard that name yet.

"She's a Day Walker like me," Kieran told her. "When I first went into the field, Caspar thought it would be better if I didn't work directly with shifters or humans. I was still a little uneasy around people."

Not much had changed in Dakota's view but she didn't say what she was thinking.

"Angel handled all the contact with anyone other than Caspar but allowed me to do tracking and to handle any problems," Kieran said then chuckled. "Back in the beginning, the Organization didn't care how we took care of paranormal killings or gaining attention from humans."

She nodded. "So I've heard."

He was still grinning. "I was good at that so Angel and I were sent out more and more all over the country. She helped track down our suspects and once we were sure that they were guilty, I took care of them. Since there are a lot more shifters out there than Walkers, we mostly ran into rogues who were breaking both human and shifter law. Our problems increased after we kept coming up with shifters whose leaders didn't want to work with Walkers. Caspar added Remy to the team so he could ease the tensions, and so the shifters didn't feel like a couple of Walkers were just hunting them down."

Oh yeah, Dakota could picture Kieran's reaction. That must have been something to see. "And yet you didn't quit."

"I'd never leave Caspar," Kieran told her. "He saved my life."

"Your boss?" Dakota questioned. "Isn't that his job?"

Kieran shook his head, which dislodged her hold. But he didn't pull away. Instead Kieran grasped her forearms and yanked her on top of him more directly. Dakota smiled. Her legs bracketed his, and his body under hers just felt right. Maybe she could even share some of her heat with him.

"Are you sure you want to know this?"

The serious tone surprised her but she didn't hesitate to nod.

"When I was eighteen years old, I was captured by a group of shifters that kept me in a cage and experimented on me," Kieran told her.

Dakota gasped. "You're the Walker they saved from Mount Fauna!" Everything fell into place. Kieran's loyalty to his boss, his feelings about shifters, and even the way he pushed people away.

Kieran jerked when she said the name of the facility where he'd been held. "So you've already heard about it?" he asked softly.

"Yes," she admitted. "It was before I joined the Organization. I was still in school and training but my uncle was on the rescuing team. He's the only one in my family I still see and he told me about it." Dakota couldn't believe it. The Mount Fauna case was the biggest investigation that anyone in her family had ever been involved with. The worst case of abuse ever recorded against a Walker from a shifter.

Her stomach rolled and she felt slightly ill. Her lover had been the one who they'd found. She could still remember the description her uncle had shared with her father.

"Your uncle?" Kieran asked.

"Yeah," she said. "You might know him from then."

"No," he replied. "I don't really remember a lot from the first days except Caspar. Everything else is still a blur, and I really try not to think about that time in my life. Ever."

She couldn't blame him. If she'd been in his shoes, she'd probably never leave her house again.

"I was just surprised when you said uncle. Most agents I've met have no contact with their family that are not also inside the Organization. Remy is the only exception that I'm aware of," Kieran said.

"My uncle is the only one I have any contact with. I've run into him on some cases in the past."

She was lucky her uncle had been on that case otherwise she wouldn't have any information at all. All records were sealed on the case. Once she was in the field, she'd tried to read about the rescue, curious about the biggest Organization rescue in history, but had been unable to get any new intel.

It was crazy to realize that Kieran had been the Walker saved from ten years of torture. Her eyes filled with tears as she thought about everything he'd been through.

Dakota sat up, still straddling Kieran's waist and cupped his face. "I'm so glad you made it out of there."

He nodded. "Caspar was the one who got me out of the cage. He took me to his house while I healed, then brought me into the Organization. I don't know what I would be doing if it wasn't for him."

"I understand," she assured him. And now they wanted Kieran to transfer away from the man who'd saved him. "Have you spoken to Caspar?" She really didn't want to tell Kieran that his boss would be taking on a very dangerous mission. Although he probably already knew if Sparro had told him about the transfer.

"Not yet," Kieran said. "I plan to call him later. I want to know about this case he's taking."

Relief swept through her. She was glad that Kieran seemed to know as much as she did.

"There's more I need to tell you," Kieran said

"Sure," she said. Anything he wanted to talk about she was willing to listen to.

"This doesn't have to do with the Organization. Or it might actually," Kieran shook his head as he spoke. "I'm not sure how all this is connected."

"Tell me," she urged. "I might be able to help."

Kieran gripped her waist as he sat up and scooted to lean against the headboard taking her with him. Once he'd settled, Kieran positioned her inside his legs up against his chest. She rested her cheek against his chest as she peered up at him.

She also suspected that he was buying himself some time. If he needed to gather his thoughts, she wouldn't rush him.

"When I found out that Caspar asked Dean to keep an eye on me, I switched hotels. You know that," Kieran said. "I picked this one from the Internet. I could have chosen any on the Strip."

"Okay," she encouraged him to continue.

"And I picked the one run by Walkers," he said.

This had to be the group that had been talking to Dean. As pissed off as she was at her partner she could see why he'd been doing what he had. Dean had never wanted the night-to-night patrols or tracking down suspects. He had loved the science classes at school and had excelled in the labs. But this wasn't just about Dean. Somehow Kieran had gotten involved.

"They're living and working right in this hotel," Kieran told her.

She fought the urge to look around. Even though they obviously wouldn't be in the suite, it still felt weird that she'd been walking among a bunch of Walkers without knowing it. She must have been really distracted by Kieran. "I still can't believe it."

"Yep, this hotel is owned, operated and run by a group of Walkers," Kieran told her.

"How many?" she asked.

"I don't really know for sure," he admitted. "I've met two so far."

"And you're okay?" she asked. Dakota ran her hands over his chest just for her own peace of mind. Kieran had been dealing with so much on top of their budding relationship.

Kieran chuckled. "As much as I can be. But here's the weird part."

"What?" She braced herself for bad news.

"The man, Walker, who owns this place I've met before," Kieran told her.

"From a past case?" she asked. "Is he dangerous?" Dean had acted like the Walkers hadn't been causing any trouble but she had rushed off without letting him explain much.

"No," Kieran said. "From Mount Fauna."

"I... You..."

"I know," Kieran said. "It's hard to think about, much less put into words."

"I didn't know Walkers had been involved," she confessed. "I thought that the entire group had been made up of shifters." And they were inside this man's hotel. "We should get out of here!"

"He wasn't with the shifters." Kieran grabbed her hands, holding her in place. "He was a prisoner like me."

"But." Dakota didn't understand. "I thought you were the only one rescued.

"I was," he said. "I thought Jack...Jackson was dead."

"Well, obviously he's not."

"No, he's very much alive. I met with him after I got back from your office," Kieran told her.

"Talk about a rough morning," she said quietly. No wonder he'd been wrapped up in his bed. Now she wished she hadn't woken him.

"Yeah," he snorted. "It's been a bit emotional."

Dakota leaned up to kiss him. "So you've learned Caspar is taking a mission, you and your partners are being transferred while he's gone and a ghost from your past showed up. Anything else?"

He lifted an eyebrow. "You mean besides you?"

She smiled. "I'm the easy part. All I want is to be with you and to help."

"You shouldn't get involved in this," Kieran told her. "I promised myself this morning that I'd let you go until I got all this figured out."

"Again, you don't have a choice," she responded.

"Even if I tell you that I suspect your partner's involved?" he asked.

"Actually, Dean told me this morning that he'd been talking to the Walkers in town. Like I said before, I had no idea," she confessed.

"I need to figure out how everything is connected," Kieran said. "Once I do I'll be able to make a decision on what I want to do."

"Do?" she questioned.

"Stay with the Organization or accept the job offer from Jackson," Kieran answered.

Kieran hadn't mentioned any other job offer. "You'd leave Caspar?" She hoped to remind him of his earlier words.

"He's leaving me," Kieran replied. "Taking a case, and I have no idea where he'll be. I don't like it and I will find out what I can but if he can leave me this easily without even talking to me, maybe it's time I moved on."

Even though she could understand why Kieran felt the way he did, Dakota knew it was pure emotion talking. Kieran had to know that the best way to keep an eye on

Caspar, even on a mission, was within the Organization. Kieran might be hurt now but when he thought things through, she was sure he'd want to know where Caspar was and what he was doing.

Also, Dakota would have to find out more about this Jackson guy and the other Walkers. She wouldn't have the same connection that Kieran had with them so she could look at his options with an open mind. As long as both job offers kept Kieran close to her. "Why don't we order some lunch and coffee and you can tell me everything about this Jackson?" she suggested. "Then we'll come up with a plan on how to figure everything else out. I have some resources I can tap into plus a few favors owed."

"You're sure you want to do this with me?" he asked.

"One hundred percent," she replied.

Kieran surprised her by lifting her up off the bed so she could straddle his lap. "Thanks," he said before he kissed her hard.

Dakota opened up to him, allowing Kieran to plunge his tongue in against hers. Well, he was already naked and it would be a waste not to take advantage. She ran her hands down along his chest as she brushed her ass over his erection. He moaned as she lifted up and sat lower on his legs. Dakota grasped Kieran's cock and stroked him several times until he was lifting his hips.

She backed her body up more while keeping her hand on him. Once she had enough room, Dakota bent and took the tip of his hard-on into her mouth. She licked around his mushroomed head before diving down and swallowing him.

Pre-cum flowed from his slit as Dakota wrapped her hand around the base of his cock while she sucked on him. Kieran moaned, and she opened her eyes to peer up at him.

He still had his back to the headboard but now his eyelids were half closed as he watched her pleasure him. Just knowing that she had every bit of his attention was beyond sexy.

Dakota relaxed her throat as she swallowed his cock down. She loved the flavor of him and having Kieran in her control. Her body felt alive and that constant electric connection seemed to spark more intensely.

Her body was flushed and she tingled with need. Dakota slipped her free hand down her body until she was fingering her clit.

"That's it, baby," Kieran encouraged with a husky voice. "Let me see you touch yourself."

Dakota moaned around the cock in her mouth and she complied with his request. While still licking and slurping at Kieran's erection, she thrust two fingers inside her pussy. She matched the rhythm of her hand with her mouth as Kieran was pumping his hips and grunting.

His hands went to her hair where he gripped her tightly, holding her up against his flesh. Kieran came, filling her mouth with his seed as she climaxed.

"Damn," she said once she'd pulled away and collapsed on the bed.

"You can say that again," Kieran told her.

The mattress dipped as Kieran sat forward and pushed her onto her back. He covered her body with his to kiss her deeply. "Shower then food and research," he said.

"Deal," she managed while his weight pinned her down.

Kieran popped up and grabbed her arm as he leaped from the bed.

"I see you feel better," she commented.

"I've got a plan," he said as he glanced over his shoulder at her. "Sort of kill all the birds with one stone."

"I really hope you don't mean that literally," she said as he yanked her forward. "And you thought of a plan while I was sucking you off? I'm rather insulted."

Kieran just laughed at her. Yes, he was getting back to the Walker she'd first met. She had liked that part of him, and if they were going to get past all this, Kieran couldn't let his emotions cloud his mind. He was too deep into what was happening and she didn't want to find him in the middle of a nightmare again.

She stepped past Kieran when they reached the bathroom and slapped his ass. "I'll turn on the water."

* * * *

The second pot of coffee had been delivered, and Kieran had laid out his plan for Dakota. She seemed skeptical but at least she agreed that getting everyone together would either get the confessions he wanted or it would be complete chaos. A knock at the door pulled his attention from his laptop. Dakota glanced up from beside him on the couch.

"That should be Remy," Kieran told her. "I wanted to talk to him first."

She nodded before she went back to digging into Caspar's last few missions he'd gone on before he'd been promoted out of the field. With her resources at the local division of the Organization, she was already making more headway than he'd have been able to do. Dakota had been right, she was already helping him.

It was a different experience from when he worked with Remy and Angel. Usually Kieran wasn't involved in the gathering of intel but he was enjoying it. Kieran strolled to the suite door. Before he even reached it, he could smell his partner's scent. Fresh grass and woodland were the aromas he was used to from Remy.

Kieran pulled the door open and smiled at his partner. "Thanks for coming."

"Of course," Remy said as he walked inside. "It looks like you got some sleep."

He nodded. "Come on in and have a seat."

Remy was staring at him. "Before you say anything, there's something I need to tell you."

Which was why Kieran had asked his partner to come by now. Remy was hiding something that Sparro had almost spilled in his office and Kieran wanted to clear the air between them before everyone else arrived. "About what

Sparro alluded to earlier?"

"Yeah." Remy turned to go further into the suite then stopped. "Oh," he said, clearly surprised when he spotted Dakota on the couch.

"Hey." Dakota waved at him.

"Hi," Remy replied before he glanced at Kieran. The look of confusion would have been funny any other time but Kieran wasn't really in a joking mood.

"This is Dakota," Kieran introduced. "She works for the local office here in Vegas."

"I...I've..." Remy rubbed the back of his neck. "I've heard about you."

Dakota stood as she raised an eyebrow. "Really?"

"I just came from your office and speaking to your partner," Remy told her.

"Ah." She nodded.

"He didn't say that you'd be here too," Remy said but he was looking at Kieran again.

"Dakota's helping me with a few things," Kieran said.

Remy sniffed. Kieran had no doubt that his partner could pick up the traces of his and Dakota's coupling. Kieran narrowed his eyes, warning Remy not to mention it. Remy shrugged his shoulder before he walked over to chair across from the couch. Kieran knew that while Remy wouldn't embarrass him in front of Dakota, his partner would still have a lot to say once they were alone.

Kieran had never been with a shifter before. Hadn't even thought it was possible for him because of his trust issues with shifters. But Dakota had changed everything he'd once believed. Even when he tried to forget what she was, Kieran couldn't. Her scent was a constant reminder, along with little mannerisms that he'd noticed. Dakota was a shifter and Kieran might be falling in love with her.

"So tell me what you've been hiding," Kieran said as he sat back down next to Dakota.

"Well, there was more to our vacation time than what we believed," Remy said.

"That much is obvious," Kieran said with a snort.

"No." Remy shook his head. "I don't mean Caspar. I didn't know about that."

"But you know something," Kieran accused.

Remy looked right into his gaze. "Before Angel left for her honeymoon, she put in a transfer to be closer to her mate's pack."

Kieran jerked back. He couldn't hold in his reaction. He felt like he'd been slapped. "She what?"

"She wants to stay in Texas with her mate, and since we travel so much, she asked to be on another team," Remy told him.

The betrayal that he felt was so strong that Kieran's heart actually ached. How had he missed all the signs that the people he'd surrounded himself with, the few he actually trusted, were ready to leave him? It hurt.

He wouldn't let anyone see how much this affected him. But this was just one more reason he might make the change and take Jackson up on his offer.

"I know what you're thinking and you're wrong. I'm not even supposed to be telling you. Angel wants to do that herself," Remy said.

Kieran snorted. Like Angel telling him in person would make a difference to the fact that she didn't want him any longer.

"She loves her mate," Remy said. "But she also loves you."

"Yeah," he scoffed. "I can tell."

"She does," Remy snapped. "And you know it. If she'd told you then, you'd have insisted we all stay together. You'd be stuck working in one place all the time and with only wolf shifters. You'd do it for her but after only a couple of weeks, you'd be miserable."

"I..." Kieran didn't know how to reply to that comment since that was exactly what he would have done. "That's what friends do."

"It is," Remy agreed. "So is what Angel is trying to do.

She doesn't want to lose either of us but she has to put her mate first."

Kieran felt Dakota slip her hand into his and squeeze. He glanced over at her. She smiled and nodded. Kieran blew out a long breath. "We could have worked something out." And they would have. Between himself, Remy and Angel, they would have come up with the best plan.

"Angel wants you to find your place in the world and she doesn't think you have yet," Remy said. He tilted his head toward Dakota and grinned at him. "Seeing you here, happy, I have to admit Angel's probably right."

Kieran pressed his lips into a tight line and didn't respond. Things might be changing for him but that didn't mean he'd 'found his place'. His feelings for Dakota were too new and he wasn't even certain where he'd be working in a week. Still, as he peered around his suite, he could admit that he was more comfortable here and with these two people than he'd ever been before in his life. Without the drama of the last few days, Kieran would have been bored out of his mind. But really, a little bit of drama at a time would have been better. Still, Remy might have a point, and Angel hadn't set out to hurt him.

"So why are you telling me now if Angel wanted to do it?" Kieran asked.

"I thought about it the entire way here. I knew you were going through something when you called. You never ask for help." Remy glanced to Dakota then back at him. "I'd pretty much already decided before I got to town but after I got the call that you broke into the office here, I knew I needed to. Now with this transfer in front of us you need all the information I know."

Kieran nodded. "I'm glad you told me."

Remy laughed. "I don't think Angel will feel the same. I spoke to her earlier and she's supposed to drive out here before she heads back to her husband's ranch."

Great. Kieran shrugged. He didn't need anything else added to his plate but it would be good to see Angel. Even if she did bring the flea bag she'd married. Fuck, he really needed to work on his shifter insults now that he was with Dakota. "We'll deal with that when we have to."

"Okay," Remy agreed easily. "Why don't you tell me what you're up to?"

Chapter Nine

Kieran paced the living room of the suite as the time inched closer to his plan being fully in place. He'd spoken to all the players and now he just had to wait.

Dakota walked back into the room from putting everything they'd been working on into the bedroom so it would be away from prying eyes. He didn't want to tip his hand before he could get started.

"You okay?" she asked quietly as she stepped up to him.

Kieran wrapped his arm around her waist and pulled her close before he glanced out at Remy, who stood on the other side of the room talking on his cell phone. Of course Kieran could hear what his partner was saying. Remy was trying to put off Angel's visit.

She was still technically on her honeymoon, and both Kieran and Remy had agreed that she didn't need to be involved in this mess. So Remy was trying to convince her that Kieran was fine and actually enjoying his own vacation. At least to hold her off for a few days until the dust had cleared and Kieran knew what he was going to do.

"I'm okay," he told Dakota, realizing that she was staring up at him when he'd failed to answer her question.

"The call to Caspar seemed to go pretty well," she said.

Kieran had given in and called his boss. He hadn't been surprised when Caspar had told him that he'd just gotten to town. Kieran had suspected that Caspar would be at his room at any time. Actually he counted on it since Caspar had a part in his plot.

Caspar had agreed to come to his suite and bring Dean with him. After he'd hung up with his boss, Kieran had phoned Jackson, asking to speak to him and Alex.

He suspected adding the Walkers to the discussion was going to complicate things but this way no one could get out of telling him what he needed to know.

"K?" Dakota cupped his face, drawing his attention back to her.

"Sorry," he said then bent and kissed her gently. "I guess my mind is wandering."

"I understand," she assured him. It felt good to know that she had his back. "But if you're not ready, we don't have to do this now."

"I do," he answered quickly. He was tired, exhausted actually, and he wanted to get back to having some fun. Screwing with the bad guys and keeping his friends on their toes. He didn't want to be on vacation any longer. It was time to get back to work. Either with the Organization or with Jackson.

"Someone's coming," Remy called out.

Kieran released Dakota's waist but gripped her shoulders. "Thank you for your help. I couldn't have gotten the information about Caspar so fast without you."

"Anytime," she replied. "And I mean that."

A knock echoed around the quiet room. The lack of scent told Kieran that it was Alex and Jackson at the door instead of his boss. He was never able to describe to a human how the lack of any scent made the Walkers stand out.

Everyone picked up traces of their environment. Something they'd held, walked past or other people that they'd encountered. That was normal. But humans and shifters also had a distinct odor added to that.

Humans didn't smell as fresh as the shifters. They actually smelled more like the type of food they'd eaten more than anything else. If they drank a lot, ate tons of red meat or were vegans, Kieran could tell. Shifters were completely different. Depending on the species that they could change into, Kieran could place most shifter species. The felines were the hardest to separate. The lions and tigers smelled different from one another, but cougars, cheetahs and jaguars confused him.

Kieran had been around wolf shifters so much that he could easily pick them out of any size crowd. Bear shifters were also easy for him to determine although some of the smaller species he didn't know at all. Most species shared a similar scent that underlined their environment. Kieran couldn't place a species he'd never scented before because he had nothing to compare it to.

"Do you want me to get the door?" Remy asked as he strolled closer.

"I'll do it," Kieran responded. He yanked Dakota forward and kissed her deeply before he straightened. She was a little breathless and that made him smile.

Another knock came, so as calmly as possible he walked to the door. Everyone who was coming would be able to pick up if he was nervous. Even though Caspar and Dean were humans, they were still highly trained agents.

Kieran pulled the door open and even though he was expecting to see Jackson, his breath still caught in his chest as he caught sight of his old friend. At first he'd told Caspar about his buddy who'd been held with him and it had made him feel better that someone else knew his buddy Jack. But as he'd started to heal, Kieran had buried his memories of Jack deep down. It hurt less that way.

"Hey, Kieran," Jackson said with a smile.

It was obvious that both Dakota and Remy were suspicious of Jackson, but looking at his old friend, Kieran had no doubt that Jackson only had good intentions.

"Hey, guys." Kieran pushed away his feelings as he greeted the two Walkers. "Come in, please."

Kieran stepped back to allow the two Walkers to step past him. If they were surprised to see two shifters already there, they didn't show it. Jackson strolled forward straight to Dakota.

"Jackson Wickham," he said as he held out his hand.

"Dakota Reese." She placed her hand on his and the smile

stayed on her face, but it was obvious to Kieran that the two of them were sizing each other up.

Alex had reached Remy and a similar scene was taking place. Kieran shook his head as he closed the door. Caspar and Dean hadn't even shown up yet. He needed to get the four of his guests to act like adults. *Fuck,* he almost groaned out loud. When had he become the voice of reason? Damn it, he wanted to go back to being the unpredictable one.

He stalked across the room to stand behind Dakota and placed his hand on her lower back, staking his claim.

Jackson nodded and stepped back.

"Let's get the introductions out of the way. And everyone put their Alpha intimidation attitudes aside," Kieran said.

"Sorry," Dakota responded.

Kieran just shook his head. She didn't need to apologize for anything.

"Dakota is special to me," Kieran said. "She knows everything."

Jackson's eyes widened before he nodded. Kieran was glad he didn't have to spell out what he meant to his old friend. He hadn't even told Remy or Angel about Mount Fauna. They knew he'd been captured and tortured but he'd never gone into detail.

"My apologies. I know how you feel about shifters and yet two are inside your suite."

"These are the only two shifters that I trust, and I do trust them," Kieran said. "This is my partner, Remy."

Alex was still standing close to Remy and even though he'd stopped trying to intimidate his partner, Kieran could see the Walker trying to hold back a sneer.

"His best friend too," Remy added.

"A wolf shifter," Alex spat.

"Yes," Remy said with a growl. "You got a problem with that?"

"What if I do?" Alex replied as he rolled his shoulders and braced his feet into a fighting stance.

"Enough!" Jackson snapped. He didn't even have to raise

his voice to have Alex and Remy both freezing in place. Jackson looked back at Kieran. "Please excuse Alex. He has a past with a pack of wolf shifters."

If anyone could understand, it was him so Kieran nodded before he turned to his partner. "Remy?"

Remy's shoulders slumped and he cleared his throat. "I'm sorry about whatever happened to you but I had nothing to do with it and neither did my pack. My family has been involved with protecting others for generations. I have nothing against Walkers." He waved a hand in Kieran's direction. "Obviously."

"Yes." Alex ran his hand over his face. "That was very rude of me. I've been around wolf shifters before. I guess I was just caught off guard. I expected to just share a couple of drinks and visit with my boss's oldest friend."

"Well, let's sit, why don't we?" Kieran offered.

"Why do I get the feeling that you asked us here for more than just catching up?" Jackson said as he strolled over to one of the chairs and sat.

Alex followed to stand behind Jackson's chair while Remy backed off until he stood against the wall. Kieran led Dakota to the couch so they could sit together.

"What are you up to, K?" Jackson questioned.

"You always could read me," Kieran told him. "So you must also know that I'd need better answers to what we spoke about earlier."

"I figured that's what you wanted to discuss," Jackson said.

"It is, among other things," Kieran hedged. He didn't want to start the conversation until everyone was there.

"You're being cagey," Jackson accused.

Behind him, Alex shifted on his feet.

Kieran had no doubt that if anyone tried to harm Jackson, Alex would attack. Luckily Kieran had two shifters on his side but he really just wanted to talk. "I'm sorry about that," Kieran said honestly. "I think I might still be in shock a little. It's not every day that a ghost comes back from the past."

"I understand that," Jackson agreed.

"Since we're on the subject," Dakota said, "why did you contact Kieran today?"

"As soon as I heard about him staying in the hotel, I made plans to return right away, and since I'd just gotten in, I had Alex find him for me," Jackson replied, peering between Dakota and Kieran. "I told you this earlier."

Kieran opened his mouth to respond but Dakota covered his knee with her hand. "Kieran had a very busy morning and your timing is rather suspicious."

"I have no idea what happened this morning," Jackson said as he sat forward in his chair and braced his elbows on his knees. He was talking to him, and Kieran believed him.

"I was just so excited and nervous to see you again I didn't want to put the meeting off any longer. I'd stayed away at your boss's request but you came to my hotel. We could have run into each other in the casino, café, bar or anywhere in town really. I didn't think that would be a good idea."

If that had happened, Kieran was certain he would have freaked out, thinking he'd lost his mind. "I'm glad you did."

"When was the last time you spoke to Caspar Westbridge?" Dakota asked.

"Not for several years." Jackson frowned and broke eye contact with Kieran. "Is this an interrogation, agent?"

"It can be," Dakota said with a smile. "And it seems you know more about me than I believed."

"Of course I do," Jackson told her. "I know everything that happens in my city with any paranormal."

"Funny," Dakota commented. "I always thought of this as my city. You know, since I'm out there every night keeping it safe and watching out for trouble."

Jackson relaxed his stance, appearing more comfortable, but Kieran didn't believe the gesture for a second. The power that radiated from Jackson was pure Alpha, and although he might not be a shifter, Jackson had an aura of dominance that surrounded him. "You do a good job keeping the streets safe. I commend what you and your Organization have done. However, this is a big town and paranormals can fall through the cracks easily. Especially ones who don't want to be noticed. I notice."

"And use your contact within my company," she said.

Kieran turned to stare at Dakota. She was a badass and her questioning Jackson showed that. She sat next to Kieran calm and in control like she had no worries in the world. When she wanted to get her point across, like at that moment, her tone was cold and hard. "Maybe we shouldn't..." he started. They weren't supposed to get into Jackson's relationship with Dean yet.

"It's okay." Jackson waved Kieran off. "I do. But you must be aware as it's your partner I speak with."

Dakota narrowed her eyes. "I didn't know until today."

"Ah," Jackson commented. "And you don't trust me."

"Maybe I don't understand why you didn't make yourself known to everyone. Dean wouldn't have kept you a secret unless you'd insisted."

"I did, as matter of fact," Jackson confirmed. "If you know Kieran's story, you have a pretty good idea about mine. I prefer to keep my business my own and have no need to get involved with any more shifters than necessary."

"So you chose Dean because he was human?" Dakota asked.

"Actually, your boss had him contact me," Jackson corrected. "But yes, I did agree to use him as my contact because he was human. You'd have to ask him why he accepted."

"I will," she said.

As she finished speaking, a knock interrupted whatever it was Alex was going to say. Alex jerked his head around to Kieran. "Are you expecting someone else?"

Kieran nodded before he stood. "Excuse me for a second." He walked quickly to the door, not wanting to leave the four of them alone for very long. At least he wasn't going out of the room so he could still keep an eye on them and hear what was being said.

As he approached the door, he caught the scent of his boss. Normally that would have put him at ease but just then Kieran had a lot of anger and confusion directed at Caspar. He pulled open the door to find the two humans he'd been expecting.

"Kieran." Caspar inclined his head.

Kieran held the door open wide. "Come in."

Caspar frowned but did step inside. Kieran knew the minute that Caspar spotted Jackson since his boss stiffened. Caspar snapped his head back to him. "I shouldn't be surprised, but you've caught me off guard."

"Why?" Kieran asked as he slammed the door. Luckily for Dean he'd followed Caspar closely so he was already in the suite. "Because you didn't think I'd find out that the only person that could possibly understand what I've been through was alive?"

"You're angry," Caspar said.

Kieran fisted his hands at his side. "Yeah, you could say that."

"So think about how you would have felt back then. We didn't know Jackson was alive until he contacted us. If I would have told you about him, you'd have given up everything you'd worked so hard for."

It was difficult to keep from hitting the man in front of him. The human who'd been like a father to him. "You mean I'd have given up what you wanted me to be."

"No." Caspar moved fast for a human and grabbed Kieran's hand. "I cared for you. I'd taken you in, taken care of you and didn't want to lose you. If you'd have left, there is no telling what would have happened to you. I didn't want to have to hunt you one day."

Kieran's hand shook where Caspar grasped it. He wanted to believe so bad but he just wasn't sure.

"K?" Dakota stepped up to his side, and he was so fucking relieved that he reached for her in front of everyone, not even caring if it made him look weak. She allowed him to wrap his arm around her shoulder. "Why don't we sit down so we can talk about this?"

"Talk about what?" Dean asked. "And why are you here? You don't need to get involved in this."

Kieran snarled at Dean for talking that way about Dakota.

"Wait!" Caspar held up a hand. "Dakota is right. We should all sit. I think we do need to discuss things. That's why you brought us all together, isn't it?"

Kieran nodded.

"Okay." Caspar dropped his hand and strolled into the living area.

It took a few moments but Dean finally followed his uncle.

Kieran turned to Dakota. He didn't want to say anything in front of the others but he hoped his eyes told her how grateful he was for her presence. The smile she gave him was beautiful and he knew she understood what he couldn't say. Then she led him back to the couch.

Caspar sat in the other chair while Dean joined Remy at the wall. Kieran sat and made sure that Dakota was close to his side.

"It's time I know everything," he said. "And I want the truth." Kieran made sure to meet every single person's gaze except for Remy's and Dakota's. When they'd all nodded, he sat back.

"Where would you like to begin?" Caspar asked.

"No place better than the beginning," Kieran stated firmly.

Dakota was so proud of Kieran and how he was handling everything. There'd been a couple of minutes where he'd faltered, and she was glad that she'd been able to be there to keep him grounded.

"I'm not sure where the beginning starts for you," Caspar admitted.

"How about the mission that brought you to finding me," Kieran said.

It had taken hours but she'd stumbled on some unsealed files that were to do with the Mount Fauna investigation. It had been the last active case that Caspar had worked.

Caspar glanced toward Jackson. "I can't talk about that."

Jackson snorted. "Like I haven't had someone hack into your files and don't already have every detail from everything written about it."

"What?" she said at the same time as Caspar.

Jackson smiled and nodded. "I have a vested interest."

She had to respect the guy. While looking into Caspar's last couple of missions, she'd also run a deep background check on Jackson. There she'd been surprised. With the amount of family money he had, Jackson didn't have to actually work. He did, though. Not only did he own businesses all over the world but he was also involved in the day-to-day operations of the companies.

"If you don't wish to share, I'll be more than happy to do so for you," Jackson said to Caspar.

"I knew you were trouble the first time I laid eyes on you," Caspar said with an angry glower.

Jackson merely shrugged, and Dakota couldn't believe it. If she'd gotten that look, she would have backed down for sure.

"Fine," Caspar sighed. "I was the head agent in charge of the Mount Fauna case. You know that but what you don't know is that there were two other locations that we'd taken down first. The way we found Mount Fauna was by some encrypted files we found from a laptop in a place much like the one we found you at in Missouri."

Kieran was so rigid that Dakota was worried that maybe she should have argued against his plan better. Having all the information come to light was a good idea but she didn't think that Kieran needed the details. She scooted closer to his side and leaned her weight against him.

"I'd been trying to find the ringleaders for three years when I found you and a stockpile of intel. I knew it would take time to go through all of the information so I took you home to help you heal," Caspar said.

"Did you get anyone else out alive?" Kieran asked.

"No," Caspar admitted. "You were the only one. We caught them by surprise and not only saved you but got all their files."

"Oh." Kieran sounded so disappointed.

"We didn't know that Jackson had survived until he called looking for you," Caspar said. "But I already explained to you why I didn't tell you."

Kieran looked toward Jackson, and Dakota was certain that the fact that Caspar had known Jackson was still alive would be the most difficult thing Kieran would have to let go of.

"About a month and a half after I brought you back, we got word from our hackers that they'd broken the code. And gotten the name of one of the organizers," Caspar explained. "It was a surprise since it was someone I knew."

"Who?" Kieran asked quietly.

"My best friend and partner at the time, Bradley Johnson. We'd gone through training together. He'd disappeared from a mission years before that and was presumed dead. It wasn't until we found the records of your...capture that we knew he was still alive," Caspar said.

Dakota looked over at her partner in shock. She couldn't even imagine what it would be like to have your partner turn on you and everything you stand for. She might be mad at Dean but she still cared for him. She also understood why Dean wanted to make a change. Even through her anger, she wished Dean the very best. He was her friend and she would always have his back. And since she'd already forgiven him, she just wanted to go over and let him know that they would never end up like Caspar and his partner. Instead she stayed seated to listen to Caspar's story.

"By the time we figured everything out, Bradley was nowhere to be found and every location we uncovered was empty," Caspar said.

"Bradley is a shifter?" Alex asked. "I found his name but

we couldn't locate his file."

"We removed all traces of Bradley from the servers. We didn't want him to get a hold of anything. With his experience with the Organization, we worried he'd find a way to access our files," Caspar said. "He's an eagle shifter."

Kieran growled. "I remember him."

"I figured you might," Caspar admitted. "I never brought it up because I felt guilty about it being my friend involved."

"So you took me in out of guilt?" Kieran questioned.

"No," Caspar said quickly. "Well, maybe at first, but after a few days I saw something in you that I knew was pure and good. After that, I concentrated on getting you trained and finding you a partner you could trust. I didn't want you to go through what I was."

Kieran nodded. "But you still kept Jackson from me."

"It was years later, Kieran," Caspar argued. "You would have left us and I didn't want anything to happen to you. You know I care about you. I just couldn't take the chance that Jackson would bring out the darkness inside you."

"You just said that Kieran was pure and good," Dakota reminded Caspar. She didn't like anyone talking about Kieran being evil or bad.

"We all have a little darkness inside us," Caspar said. He waved his hand in Jackson's direction. "Jackson didn't even remember Kieran at first. And his escape was suspicious." Caspar glanced toward Jackson. "No offense."

"I understand," Jackson replied. "That is the reason I agreed to stay away from K."

"I still think I should have been consulted. Especially after so much time had passed," Kieran said. "But there is nothing I can do about it now. What I want to know is, why this elaborate plan to get me here? I know everyone in this room is connected. And I want to know what's going on."

Caspar chewed on his lips, watching Kieran for a few moments before he nodded. "Sparro told you about me going back into the field."

"Yes, and—"

"Wait," Caspar said when Kieran started to interrupt. "I have to finish what I started. I've waited years to find Bradley and we have the best tip we've ever gotten. It has to be me that brings him in."

"Why?" Kieran asked.

"It's the only way I can make it up to you that my partner, my best friend, is responsible for everything you went through," Caspar said simply.

"I don't need that," Kieran argued. "It can be someone else."

"I need it," Caspar whispered.

Kieran sighed. "Fine but why do you have to transfer us?"

Caspar smiled. "You can't run around wild, and I have no idea how long I'll be in the field. I trust Sparro more than anyone else to be able to manage you."

"You act as if I have no control," Kieran accused.

Caspar raised an eyebrow. "If you want to, you have the most control of anyone I've ever seen. But if you want to cause trouble no one would be able to stop you. Not even Remy. Hell, sometimes I think you've corrupted Remy instead of his calm influence rubbing off on you."

"I'm not a child," Kieran bitched.

"You broke into the office here, attacked my boss, got yourself locked up, and that's just what I know about," Caspar pointed out.

"You had me followed!" Kieran claimed.

"I did." Caspar sat forward. "You're like a son to me. I would do anything to make sure you were protected. I knew Jackson was here, and that as soon as he learned about your presence in town, he'd find you. I wanted to make sure you were okay."

"You *suggested* I come here, knowing that Jackson would find me?" Kieran repeated. "How does that make sense?"

"If you needed help, I knew you trusted him. If I'm not able to watch out for you, at least someone could. Someone who had no connection to the Organization. That way you didn't only have to rely on your partner and other agents."

"So you trust me?" Jackson asked.

"I've kept my eye on you," Caspar told him. "Which I'm sure you're aware of. If you haven't turned against the humans or shifters you're around yet I have to hope you won't."

Jackson nodded. "And if I steal your boy away from you?"

"What?" Caspar questioned.

"I offered Kieran a job with me. If he accepts, he can choose where he wants to go. And it'll keep him out of danger," Jackson replied.

Caspar glanced at Kieran before he laughed. "Kieran can decide where he wants to go and I'll support him. He is one of the few agents that can make the decision to leave since he wasn't commissioned by his bloodline."

"But?" Jackson asked.

"He's not going anywhere," Caspar said as he looked between Kieran and Dakota.

"I'm sitting right here," Kieran snapped. "And again, I am *not* a child."

"Of course not," Caspar agreed with a playful tone. "But are you going to leave Remy alone? Or your new girlfriend? How are you going to manage to keep your mind off what I'm doing if you don't have access to my case? I've already gotten Sparro's permission for you and Remy to be my contacts while I'm in the field."

Jackson sighed. "Well played."

Dakota pressed her lips together to keep from smiling. The way that Caspar and Jackson were fighting over Kieran amused her while making her feel good that someone else cared about him. So far both of Kieran's options kept him close to her so she hadn't complained. No one had questioned her claim on him.

"I'm not abandoning you," Caspar said to Kieran. "It doesn't matter what is changing for you. I'll always do what I have to so that you're protected."

"I appreciate it," Kieran responded with a small smile. "I don't know what I want to do right now but I probably won't leave the Organization." He looked at Jackson. "Sorry."

Jackson shrugged. "I just want to see my friend. If you stay in town, I'll still get to see you." Jackson grinned. "As matter of fact, you'll need a place to live. And I happen to have this suite or a bigger one that I would give to you. At no cost."

Kieran's eyes widened and he looked at Dakota. She nodded. She knew how comfortable Kieran was here. She was as well. And she planned to spend plenty of time with him. It might be too soon to move in together, it definitely was, but that didn't mean they would sleep apart. She still had her room so she could shift and they could each have their space when needed.

"So?" Jackson asked.

Kieran looked away from her, and Dakota held back a frown. With everything out in the open, she was ready to be alone with her man.

"I'll take you up on your offer. At least until I find a more permanent place," Kieran said. "Thank you."

"Of course, that's what friends do. We have some sites that have a kitchenette and more square feet," Jackson offered.

Kieran shook his head as he linked his fingers with hers. "I'll stay in this one for now. I have good memories here."

Damn, Dakota knew she was blushing but since Jackson chuckled and nodded she didn't mind.

"I know it'll take time for everyone to trust one another," Caspar said. "But I think this is going to work out."

Dakota agreed. She ran her thumb over the pulse on Kieran's wrist. He was more relaxed now than he'd been before.

"How about a drink?" Kieran offered. "Remy ran out and grabbed a nice bottle of Scotch."

"Sure," Caspar agreed.

"Thanks," Jackson said.

Kieran rose and headed to the desk where they'd set

the alcohol and glasses earlier. Remy followed him over. Dakota took the opportunity to stroll over to her partner.

"Still sure you want to get involved in all of this?" Dean asked her.

He was smiling but she could pick up a faint trace of nervousness from him. She patted his shoulder. "No doubt in my mind."

"I was going to tell you," he said. "I wanted to tell you everything."

"I know," she said. "And I understand that you had to do what Caspar and Sparro asked. I'm not mad anymore."

"You're not?" he questioned with what had to be hope blooming on his face.

"You never wanted the field like I did. I'm glad that you'll be able to go into the labs and use your brain."

"I am too," he admitted.

Dakota laughed. "Besides, maybe you'll make some brilliant research find and become rich and famous. I need a new car."

"Sure." Dean nodded. "I'll get right on that."

"Good," she told him.

"We're okay?" he asked.

"Yes," she agreed quickly. "As long as I still get to see you."

"Well, we still have to have our *Supernatural* nights," he said.

"Right!" Dakota agreed. Every Thursday that they had the night off, she and her partner would get together at one of their houses and watch their favorite television show. On the nights they had to work, they recorded it to watch when they could. But they never missed an episode or watched it without the other.

"As long as your man doesn't mind," Dean said tilting his head at Kieran as he approached.

"I think that can be arranged," Kieran said as he joined them. He held out two crystal glasses that Remy had purchased. The wolf shifter had stated that the Scotch he'd bought could only be enjoyed from proper drinking glasses.

Dean accepted the alcohol. "So, no hard feelings?"

Kieran laughed. "Of course not." He clinked his glass with Dean's. "Besides, my second favorite pastime is fucking with the lab nerds. You have no idea how much I can break a piece of equipment. It's like technology hates me. So that'll be fun."

Dean choked on the liquid he'd just swallowed. Remy walked up and pounded on his back.

"The sad thing is he's not joking," Remy told Dean.

While the men were distracted, Dakota leaned over to whisper into Kieran's ear. "Your second favorite? What's the first?"

Kieran kissed her on her temple. "As soon as everyone leaves I'll show you."

Dakota purred as she rubbed her face against Kieran's neck. She *really* wished their guests would leave soon. She wanted some alone time with Kieran and she had no interest in talking.

"A toast," Caspar called as he lifted his glass.

They turned toward the boss. Kieran kept his hand on her lower back to only slide it down out of everyone else's view to rub her ass.

"To new opportunities," Caspar said peering at her and Kieran.

"New opportunities," they repeated.

Dakota tapped her drink to her lover's. "And so much more," she whispered to him.

Chapter Ten

Dakota led Kieran by the hand into the bedroom. The drinks had turned into having dinner catered as everyone got to know one another better. She'd been dying to get Kieran alone but as the night had worn on, she'd noticed that Kieran had grown more and more subdued and pale.

At one point in the evening, she'd overheard Kieran and Remy arguing about the fact that Kieran needed blood. Kieran had sworn he'd taken some earlier in the day but Remy had tried to insist that Kieran drink from him.

If Caspar hadn't interrupted, Dakota didn't know what would have happened. But now that they were alone, she was going to get Kieran to drink from her. He'd refused her offer before but she was not going to let it go this time.

"God, I'm tired," Kieran said as they entered the bedroom.

Perfect opportunity. "You're hungry. You need to feed," she said.

Kieran let go of her hand and stalked away. "Don't you start on me too. I know when I need blood and I just had some this morning."

"And then had one of the most emotional days of your life. Full of ups and downs," Dakota pointed out.

"I'm fine," Kieran insisted as he yanked his shirt over his head.

Dakota strolled over as she took in the faint scars on his back. The reminder of his time in captivity was hard for her to see. Normally a Walker wouldn't have scars. Only in the most extreme cases where the Walker hadn't had a chance to heal properly did physical evidence end up not fading away. While the thin lines crisscrossed his back and shoulders, they were almost unnoticeable. Still, it made her heart ache to see them.

She ran her hand over one of the thickest lines. He stiffened.

"I don't need sympathy," he said.

"I know," she replied before she leaned forward and placed her lips against the raised flesh.

Kieran turned slowly and wrapped his arms loosely around her. "They're ugly, you don't have to touch them."

Dakota smiled. "They're a part of you so I won't ignore them. You're a survivor, Kieran, and you should be proud."

"Proud?" he repeated. "What, that I didn't die when I should have?"

"Don't say that," she told him.

"Why not?" he asked. "It's true. Until Jackson arrived I prayed for my body to finally give up so I could just sleep. I didn't care if I ever woke up."

"I'm glad you did wake up," she said as she cupped his face. "Otherwise you wouldn't be here with me."

Kieran shook his head. "Just ignore me. I'm tired."

"And hungry."

He tried to pull away but Dakota grasped his arms. She might not be as strong as him but she was a shifter so he would have to work to break her hold. She knew he wouldn't take the chance of hurting her.

"Please don't," he whispered.

Dakota didn't understand. Why was this so hard for him? "I know you can feed without killing. Why won't you drink from me?"

"I'm scared," he said quietly.

"Of?" she asked with a gentle tone.

"What if I lose control and hurt you?" he asked.

"You won't," she assured him.

"You don't know that," he argued.

"I do," she said. "I trust you."

"I haven't earned your trust. I can't take the chance," he said.

"You have to," Dakota encouraged. "I'm not going anywhere, and you need to drink. What if there was an emergency?"

"I'd take blood from Remy. He doesn't mind and I never hurt him," Kieran told her.

"If you can drink from him, why won't you take from me?" she asked.

"I hate that I have to drink from anyone. It makes me feel weak to have to depend on someone else for something that is essential."

"But if it's essential you have to feed, I'm offering," she said. "I would rather you take my blood than someone else's."

"You don't understand," he replied. "It's even harder for me to think about drinking from you than Remy."

"Why?" she asked.

"Because I don't feel the same way about Remy as I do you," Kieran admitted.

Dakota smiled. "Yeah?"

"Yes," Kieran said. "I don't want you to hate me. I don't care what other people think, I never have. But I don't want you to ever think badly about me."

"I won't," she promised. She leaned forward and brushed her lips over his. His eyes were damp when she pulled away to look up at him. "But I want this. I want to share this with you."

Kieran sighed. "If this pushes you away, I don't know what I'll do."

"Trust me," she told him. "That's all you have to do."

"Okay," he agreed.

"Good," she said before she kissed him again.

Kieran pulled her close to his body and devoured her.

Dakota opened to grant him access and melted into his hold. She loved it when he ran his strong hands down her back and cupped her ass. He lifted her off her feet, and Dakota wrapped her legs around his waist.

He strolled forward as Dakota sucked on his tongue.

He stumbled a little, and she laughed, having to pull her mouth away.

"Get me to the bed," she ordered.

"I'm trying," he said with a laugh. "I'm so fucking hard it's difficult to walk."

Dakota wiggled her hips so that she pressed against his erection. He groaned and tripped. She squeaked as they fell onto the mattress, with Kieran's weight pinning her down.

"Fuck," Kieran grumbled after they'd landed hard. "That's not what I meant to do."

Dakota ran the bottom of her feet over the back of his legs. "I'm not complaining," she said. "This way I get to touch all of you."

"Yeah," he said as he pushed forward. His cock brushed against her pussy, and they both moaned.

"Naked, we need to be naked," she urged.

"Wait," Kieran told her. "If you want me to drink from you, I want to do that first."

"Or during," she told him.

"No," Kieran said sharply. "Every Walker knows never to take blood when they're making love. That's something that is only done in books and movies."

"Oh." She was kind of disappointed.

"Just lie there," Kieran ordered as he stood back up.

"I like where this is going already," she teased.

Kieran grinned down at her before he ran his hand over the hem of her shirt and pushed the fabric up. Dakota lifted her arms to assist him. It wasn't long before she was bared for him.

"Now you," she said.

Kieran stepped back and removed his shoes, socks and pants. His erection bobbed in front of her, and Dakota couldn't help but reach for him.

"Not yet," he said as he grabbed her wrist. "If you touch me now, I won't make it to the really fun parts."

Dakota stuck her lip out in a pout. Kieran laughed then nipped her bottom lip, causing her to gasp.

"That's what you get for teasing," he told her. "Now sit up for me."

She gave him a heavy sigh but complied. Excitement coursed through her as he sat beside her on the bed. Dakota tilted her neck to the side. He chuckled.

"What now?" she asked.

Kieran shook his head. "Don't ever let anyone drink from your neck. The chance of the bite turning fatal is too high."

"There sure are a lot of rules," she complained.

"Just trying to keep you safe," Kieran told her.

"It's not just me, though, is it?" Dakota asked.

"No," Kieran answered. "We're taught by our families how to take blood. We are never to kill or our life is forfeit."

He hadn't ever mentioned his family before.

"Who taught you?" she asked.

"My father," Kieran told her. "But let's not talk about that right now."

"Okay," Dakota agreed.

Kieran held her hand gently before lifting it. Dakota laughed, she couldn't help it. "What?" he asked, clearly in surprise.

"I was picturing a completely different scenario," she admitted.

"Not as romantic as you thought?" he guessed.

"Yeah," she agreed.

"I know." Kieran raised her hand and placed a kiss across her fingers before he released her.

"What are you doing?" she asked him.

"We don't have to do this," he said. "I know it's not going how you wanted."

"K?" She grabbed his hand. "You're not getting out of this."

"I really am fine," he said. "And Jackson has even offered to let me use one of his donors if I need it. I prefer to hunt for myself but I'm taken care of."

"Hunt?" she asked. Dakota knew that Kieran didn't kill people but hunting sounded serious. When she was in her jaguar form and hunted, she always caught her prey. Usually a small rabbit or something similar.

"I use the bad guys that I capture to get my blood. When I feed people can have negative reactions. Remy usually gets a headache and humans might get nauseous. I would rather the effects hit someone I didn't care about."

"That makes sense and is sort of perfect," she told him.

Kieran grinned. "I've always thought so."

"That doesn't mean that I don't still want to do it," Dakota said. "I want to share this with you."

"If you're sure," Kieran said.

"I am," she replied.

This time when Kieran lifted her hand to his mouth, Dakota was mesmerized by the way his blue eyes brightened and glowed. His fangs dropped down but she wasn't afraid. Instead she used her free hand to grip his upper thigh. She might not be able to touch his cock but she'd be damned if she would stop from touching him at all.

Kieran closed his eyes and moaned as he licked her inner wrist. She shuddered mentally, urging him to just do it. Kieran kissed and nibbled on her skin until Dakota was panting and wriggling around.

"Kieran, do it," she pleaded.

"I will," he promised. "Just relax."

"I am," she told him. "Please…"

"Lie back," Kieran said.

Dakota let her body fall against the soft mattress.

"Close your eyes," he ordered next.

"I want to watch you," she argued but did follow his directions.

"Feel my tongue?" he asked.

"Uh-huh," she answered. Kieran was running his tongue up and down and along the veins in her wrist. Each swipe made the spark between them build until Dakota wondered if the little hairs on her body were standing up.

"With your free hand, I want you to touch yourself," he said.

"I thought you said no sex during this," she said then bit her lip. Why in the hell was she arguing with him? Dakota trailed her finger down her chest while spreading her legs open.

Kieran's cool hand grabbed her closest leg and pulled it over his lap so she was opened and bared.

"You know what I want you to do," Kieran stated firmly.

She arched her back as she pierced her pussy with two fingers.

"In and out," Kieran demanded.

Dakota hissed but started to ride her fingers. Kieran's mouth came down onto her wrist again but this time his fangs pierced her flesh. She gasped while lifting her hips to try to get her digits deeper as Kieran sucked out her blood.

Each time he drew the blood, Dakota could swear that she felt the pull on her clit.

"Oh God," she moaned. "More."

She began to shake as her body grew hot and tight. Dakota didn't even notice that Kieran was no longer taking her blood until his mouth covered hers. She wrapped her arms and legs around him while Kieran pressed his cock against her pussy.

"Yes," she hissed as he thrust inside. Dakota screamed when her climax hit sooner than she'd expected.

Kieran linked his fingers with hers before he placed her arms over her head. He plunged deep and fast, stealing her breath. He was pure need, and Dakota wanted more.

"Fuck me," she panted out. "Claim me."

Kieran roared and threw his head back as he climaxed. His fangs were still extended and he looked dangerous and sexy. Dakota peered up at him and was amazed that she could call him hers.

"Damn, every time we're together it's even better." He flexed his hips, and she was surprised to find him still hard even though she could feel his cum from his orgasm just minutes before.

With a wicked smile, Dakota rolled them until she

straddled Kieran's waist on top. She lifted herself up before she dropped back down. Kieran groaned.

"Let's test your theory," she told him.

"It might take us a couple times just to be certain," Kieran said as he planted his feet on the mattress then thrust up.

Dakota let her head drop back. "I agree."

* * * *

Kieran pulled on his black boots as he watched Dakota dress on the other side of the room. After spending the rest of their weekend in bed, it was hard to watch her cover that magnificent body. Or he was just hard. Either way he took a step forward to stop her progress.

"No," she said without even turning around.

"What?" he asked innocently.

"I can hear your feet moving," Dakota said. "You stay over there."

"I was just going to offer to help you," he told her.

"I need to put my clothes on," Dakota responded while laughing. "Not take them off."

"You're no fun," he complained.

"And you're going to make us late," Dakota replied as she spun around. Her eyes widened and she licked her lips.

Pleased with her reaction, Kieran stood straighter and preened just a little. He liked the way that her gaze went up and down his body. It was almost like he could feel it. "What were you saying about being late?" he asked.

"Damn it!" she glared at him. "You're wearing that on your first day?"

Kieran glanced down at his clothes. He wore dark black jeans that hugged his thighs, but he would be able to run in them if necessary, along with a red T-shirt on top of a white long sleeve Henley. He'd completed his wardrobe with his old, beaten-up black combat boots. He thought he looked decent enough. "Well, I'm not wearing a suit," he said.

"You don't have to look so good," she said with a frown.

Was she jealous? Kieran smiled. "You don't like it?" he asked as he ran his hand over his stomach, pulling the fabric tight.

"I hope you get patrol down in the tunnels or at the sewer plant," she told him.

Kieran laughed before he stalked toward her. "You have an evil streak," he accused.

"Remember that," she said, then pushed up and kissed him hard.

As Kieran started to pull her close, she backed away and patted his chest. "Let's go before you manage to distract me."

"Fine," Kieran said with a sigh.

He liked that she was smiling as she walked out of the bedroom. It felt like a brand-new life, being able to wake up with her before they both went into the office. He hoped that he and Remy found some action tonight. A good fight would just top off his day.

Kieran followed Dakota into the living space where she was gathering the rest of her stuff. "Are you coming back here after our shift?" he asked.

"I was planning on it," she told him.

"Good." He nodded. "Remy left me a message that Angel and her mate should be here in the morning. After we get some sleep, I'd like to meet them for lunch and wanted you to come."

"I'd love to meet her," Dakota told him.

"Good." He nodded before he walked over to the table where he'd dropped his wallet and keys.

"Are you nervous?" she asked when she came up behind him.

"About seeing Angel? Nah, I'm pretty sure that she is aware that I know. And she's right. I would have stayed with her, and in a couple months would have been bored out of my mind. Plus I would have never have come here and met you or found Jackson again," Kieran said.

"I'm glad you did," Dakota said. "But I meant at starting

at a new division."

Kieran scoffed. Was she serious? He glanced over his shoulder and saw that Dakota was watching him with her brows furrowed. She was! "You know I couldn't give a flying fuck about anyone at your office other than you. As long as I get to check on Caspar's status, I do my job and don't need anyone other than my partner."

Dakota shook her head. "I think you're going to find things run very differently here."

Kieran just shrugged. He opened the door and let her exit first. "It's not like I haven't met half the people who work with you. Dean's had them following me the entire time. I can't wait to get my payback on them."

"Hey!" Dakota said. "They were just helping out their friend. They're all good guys."

"Then they need better friends," Kieran said. "Besides if they can't stand the heat they should stay out of the kitchen."

"Oh God!" Dakota groaned. "That was terrible."

Kieran laughed. Yeah, it had been corny but he liked his little sayings. They drove Remy crazy too.

"You're going to turn my office into total chaos," Dakota said.

"Of course I am," Kieran agreed. "That's what makes this job fun." He laced his fingers in hers as they walked to the elevator. Kieran pressed the button with his free hand while Dakota just stared at him. "What?"

"Could you just try not to break anyone the first week you're there?" she asked.

"I promise," he replied.

The elevator opened, and they stepped inside. The ride down was quiet but it was a comfortable silence. When the door opened on the casino, the loud cling of the slots and people talking had him scowling.

He loved living in the hotel but he could really do without the crowds of the casino. He followed behind Dakota, keeping his gaze on her ass and ignoring everyone else. Dakota had on a pair of gray slacks with a bright-blue button-down shirt. He liked the way the cotton pants framed her pert butt.

"Eyes up, buddy."

Kieran snapped his head to the side and saw Jackson strolling toward them. He smiled at his old friend. "As long as I'm the only one looking it's all good."

Jackson laughed. "It's good to see you." He held his hand out to shake.

"Yeah, sorry I didn't return your call." Kieran glanced at Dakota. "We stayed in the last couple of days to relax."

"No problem," Jackson said. "Hey, Dakota."

"Hi, Jackson," she greeted then turned to Kieran. "Why don't I get the car pulled around and meet you out front?"

Kieran nodded and smiled. "Thanks."

The two of them waited until Dakota had disappeared into the mass of people before Jackson spoke.

"I just can't get over the fact that you're with a shifter," Jackson said.

Kieran narrowed his eyes.

"I don't mean anything bad by it. I've tried to move on myself but I still get flashbacks sometimes," Jackson said.

"I do too, and before I met Dakota, I couldn't have ever imagined I'd be with a shifter this way. But the very first night I saw her there was just something that made me want her so bad," Kieran explained. "I thought I could fight it, for about five minutes, but Dakota wouldn't allow me to push her away."

"You're a lucky man," Jackson told him.

"I know," Kieran agreed.

"I thought maybe we could get dinner one night this week. The three of us. I'd like to get to know her too," Jackson said.

"We'd like that," Kieran agreed.

"Great." Jackson grinned.

"I don't know my schedule yet but I can get back to you," Kieran told him.

"Cool," Jackson said. "I'll let you get to work then."

Kieran slapped his buddy on the back. "I'll be seeing you then."

"Oh, I got Remy set up in a room last night. I figured it would be easier being close together."

"Thanks," Kieran said with sincerity.

"And if you guys need any help with Caspar's case, I have some of my own research," Jackson told him.

"On Bradley?" Kieran asked.

"On all of Mount Fauna and the other places," Jackson said.

"I'd like to take a look at it," Kieran decided. He'd never researched his own case, but maybe it was time. Kieran had buried it all down deep, but with the support he had it was time to finally heal all his old wounds.

"I'll arrange for you to have copies of my files," Jackson told him.

"All right," Kieran said. "I better go before I make us any later."

"Have a good first day," Jackson called as Kieran waved.

Dakota was already outside waiting in her SUV by the time he stepped out. If he was staying in Vegas, and it looked like he was, he needed to get a bike. He'd really enjoyed the one that he'd borrowed. Not that he didn't want to drive in with Dakota but he wouldn't mind exploring the town on his own.

He pulled open the passenger door and climbed inside. "Jackson would like to have dinner this week."

"That would be good," Dakota said.

"You just want to interrogate him again," Kieran accused.

Dakota shrugged but was smiling. "Whatever needs to be done." She drove out of the hotel parking lot and turned into traffic.

"Do you like working nights?" he asked. As much as the two of them had already been through, there was still so much that he didn't know about Dakota.

"I guess," she said. "I've been doing it so long that it just feels natural to me. I have no problem sleeping during the day."

Kieran didn't either. "So are you going to go by your place before you come back to my suite?" he questioned.

"I already told you I was staying the night again," she said.

"I know," Kieran told her. Damn, how should he word his request? Fuck it, he was a blunt guy so why beat around the bush? Dakota already liked him. "If you wanted to go by your place and grab some more clothes, we could do that after our shift. Maybe enough for the week. I wouldn't mind seeing where you live either."

Dakota glanced at him. "Sounds good to me."

Kieran relaxed into the leather seat and peered out of the window. His new city was bright and happening. A woman in a miniskirt was dancing on the side of the road while a small three-piece band played.

Across the street from her, three young teenagers were riding skateboards right in the middle of the strip. His town was full of eccentric people. If he had to be surrounded by way too many people, at least these guys here would amuse him.

With his luck, he and Remy would probably get the patrol of the worst part of town but Kieran was actually looking forward to it.

Before Kieran realized it, Dakota had driven away from the excitement of the Strip to the building that they used for a cover. She didn't pull up to the front but instead drove around to where the guard was on duty, blocking the entrance to the parking garage.

"He needs to keep an eye out for someone trying to sneak inside," Kieran commented as Dakota slowed.

She snorted. "I think they're more worried about people trying to escape, not breaking in."

"That's the first problem," Kieran commented.

Dakota came to a stop then rolled down her window. The guard bent and peered inside the vehicle.

"Hey, Dakota."

"Hi, Charlie," Dakota said. "This is Kieran, he's a new agent."

Charlie nodded. "I've been warned."

Kieran growled and bared his fangs.

"Fuck!" Charlie said as he went pale and scrambled away. He hit the button to raise the lever, allowing Dakota to drive through.

Dakota sighed as Kieran laughed loudly. "You didn't have to scare him."

"I love this!" Kieran slapped his hands together and rubbed them. "I am going to have so much fun!"

"Shit," Dakota muttered as she pulled into her parking space. "I hope they upped their insurance."

That sent Kieran into even more laughter. He wiped the tears from his eyes before he finally got control. Yeah, he was really enjoying the twists and turns his life was taking. He lifted Dakota's hand and placed a kiss on the back of it. He'd corrupt her in no time at all and he knew she was going to enjoy every second of it.

Pack Alpha

Excerpt

Chapter One

Marissa took a drink of the coffee she'd picked up at the last gas station. The hot liquid burned her tongue and tasted like slug. It wasn't Starbucks that was for sure. She had flown into the Texas International Airport and rented a car to drive the rest of the way to the small town her sister called home. Her mind was busy thinking about how her sister Elizabeth had been so excited about moving here, but looking at the passing scenery of trees, trees, and more trees, Marissa didn't get it. It was so big and wide. No buildings, other cars, or people around.

Rolling her window down and turning Bon Jovi even louder on the stereo, she concentrated on the drive — not the reason for coming. She dreaded going into Pack territory, but Elizabeth was the only family she had left, and after finding her mate, Elizabeth wanted Marissa there for the mating ceremony.

That thought brought a smile to Marissa's face as she glanced at the invitation on the seat next to her. She wanted Elizabeth to be happy, and Greg sounded like a nice guy. She'd spoken to him numerous times on the phone, and he'd always been respectful towards her. And that wasn't common. A were who couldn't shift was an outsider. And everyone except Elizabeth had treated her that way her entire life.

Marissa had left the Pack she'd been raised in as soon as she could. Never to step foot on any Pack territory again. That was until later today. Elizabeth, on the other hand, had stayed until she met Greg, a member of a different Pack. After the initial meeting, he had offered her a teaching position at the elementary school and she had taken it. He had been courting her ever since with the blessing of her new , Gage Wolf.

Marissa chuckled, thinking of everything Greg had done to win her sister's heart. He'd known he wanted Elizabeth and had patiently waited. It had taken Elizabeth a year to agree to the mating ceremony, but she finally did. Marissa knew one of the reasons Elizabeth had been holding off was because of her.

Marissa had the same instincts as any other were and with that came the need of a Pack, but she had given up on that a long time ago. She'd grown up alone and would always remain that way. In the middle between a shifter and a human. She had many gifts due to her genes — the extended life span, the wolf traits, and some enhanced features — but not enough.

But Marissa would put everything she had into this week and the ceremony that meant so much to her sister.

The differences between her and Elizabeth had grown as they had aged. That was why Marissa had never visited Elizabeth's new home. She wasn't scared being in Pack territory; she just didn't want to face all the males and their egos. And from what she understood, the Pack's Alpha or leader was pretty young himself.

When around other wolves, the female wolf inside her demanded she mate with one of her own kind. So, as long as she avoided everyone except her sister as much as she could and kept her urges inside, everything would be okay. She would not act like the wolf she couldn't shift into.

And if the Alpha was anything like her old one, she'd just tell him where to stick it. The idea of telling the Alpha of a territory to go to hell made her smile wider and laugh harder. She wasn't seventeen anymore. She wasn't a scared little girl who had to follow everything someone told her. No, she was a grown woman. And she was going to enjoy the time with her sister.

She wasn't dressed to impress the Alpha or any men in the territory as she currently wore a pair of hip-hugging jeans and a tight pink T-shirt. The paint on her toe nails matched the colour of her shirt, as did the flip-flops. It was a far cry from the suit she wore everyday as an office assistant. She felt free.

When she almost missed the turn off to the territory gate and turned the car sharply to the left, the back of the car skidded around and kicked up dirt. Laughing, she straightened the car and slowed her speed. She didn't think Gage Wolf would be happy if she took out a couple of trees.

When she reached the gate, she stopped and waited for the guard. He didn't disappoint. A man over six feet came over to the window and leaned down, smiling at her.

"Can I help you?" he asked in a husky voice.

More books from
Crissy Smith

Enforcing his control never felt better.

It's going to be a rough week for the agents of the Birds of Prey shifter division.

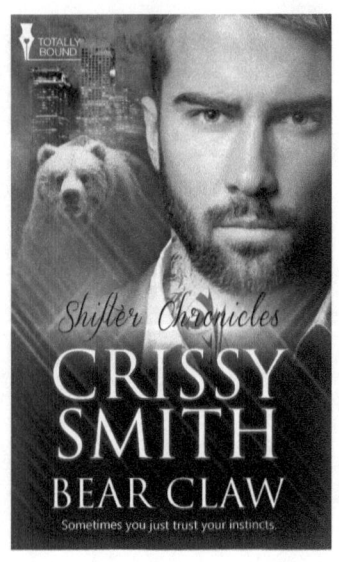

When what's on the outside doesn't match the inside,
sometimes you just trust your instincts.

Jo Black went in search of a vampire…and finding one is going to rock her world.

About the Author

Crissy Smith

Crissy Smith lives in Texas with her husband, daughter, and three Labrador retrievers. The three dogs love to curl up under her computer desk and nap while she writes. It doesn't leave a lot of room for her but what's a woman to do?

When not writing or reading, she enjoys hunting, camping and shooting. But she has a girly side too and is addicted to pedicures and coffee.

She has been writing since she was a teenager and still loves everything to do with the paranormal. Her stories and characters all have a place in her heart. She loves the alpha male, the dominant werewolf, or the Master vampire which find their way in most of her books.

Learn more about the characters she has created at her website where they have their very own page. It will be updated from time to time to let you know what's going on with them. Also you can find out who will be in the next book.

Crissy Smith loves to hear from readers. You can find contact information, website details and an author profile page at https://www.totallybound.com/